ROMANCE

Michael Connor

Michael (signature)

Ouen Press

First published in Great Britain 2012 by

Ouen Press
Suite One, Ingles Manor, Castle Hill Avenue
Folkestone, Kent, UK
www.ouenpress.com

ISBN: 978-0-9573107-0-4

A CIP catalogue record of this book is available from the British Library.

Printed in Great Britain by Marston Book Services Limited, Oxon, OX11 7AW.

Cover image from an original painting by Andrew James RP,
www.andrewjamesartist.co.uk

With thanks to
all my good friends throughout Africa

ACKNOWLEDGEMENTS

My thanks to Paula at Ouen Press for her continuing support and understanding, theabsolutegallery.com and my son Laurence for the use of his inspirational photographs at the launch, and to my very good friend Andy for painting the picture that formed the basis of the cover.

CONTENTS

CHAPTER ONE

Romance always prayed for God's intervention. To act as a chinois. To sieve out the lumps. She would ask for everything to be fine.

Joyous, the hymn rang out from the mouths of the congregation dressed all in their pressed Sunday best. Store owners, grave-diggers, members of the local council, some of the good, a few of the decidedly wayward, some deserving, some deserving less or not at all, most with their wives and children. No unaccompanied men, a modicum of lone women.

'We plough the fields and scatter
The good seed on the land'

The familiar words echoed tunefully above the sound of the small electric organ, played by a wizened, grey-haired jazz pianist who found Sunday mornings difficult and no mornings easy. They were all gathered in the compact chapel. Romance stood in her usual place at the end of the cushionless, bottom-polished wooden pew, three rows from the back. She watched a mother in a flowery frock, white with blooms of red, blue and yellow, discreetly shake an offspring for an unseen misdemeanour. She smiled gently, her concentration drifting in and out.

The Sunday service was as busy as ever, but not without spaces unoccupied approaching the front. They did not beckon; Romance was situated where she felt comfortable. Her voice could not be distinguished above the others, even at close quarters. She sang alto quite tunefully, book in hand, and her words were not simply mouthed, as was the habit of the tall, lean woman standing to the right of her, as was usual, smelling, as was also usual, of strongly perfumed soap. Soap that Romance could not afford or, in truth, cost more than she was prepared to expend on washing, and the attraction such scent would have drawn to her. From this position, with nobody to her left, Romance was still unable to see the preacher standing in the centre, before a simple altar draped in a starched white cloth secured by intricately carved heavy wooden candlesticks. But this did not bother her. It was not that the man in the pew directly in front was particularly tall or of powerful bulk. No, it was simply that Romance was particularly short; a round, slightly reserved little person with the pleasant hint of a smile in her eyes that normally went unnoticed, as holding another's gaze was something she would tend to avoid. The preacher's voice on the other hand was large, both in song and prayer, the message carried on gales of breath blasting past her to the closed iron-studded oak doors and beyond. His stare was direct and unflinching, not threatening, but – as many people judged – his stance demanded obedience.

She prayed silently with some sort of conviction, to the Lord, in bed most nights, and in church every Sunday without exception. This stone building, plain in architecture, with its standard Christian service and Methodist spartan overtones, was her selected place of Sunday worship. This was one of the few occasions when she met with people who were not work colleagues. In her village, some full day's bus journey to the north, the church was of wooden clapboard construction, and the service style referred to by many as 'happy clapping' was not really to her liking. It was many months since she had shared in that jubilant congregation. There was also the rare occasion when she found herself in the city, attending service in the cathedral: a large, overpowering structure whose dim cavernous insides seemed to devour her without either warmth or love. Where she stood now, she believed, suited best her acknowledgement of her God.

A silent prayer, the final prayer of the service was designed to allow the preacher to hasten from the front to the back, heading off the anxious to leave; duty done. He moved with speed, looking at Romance as he passed, head turning slightly. She did not meet his eyes, keeping her look low, and from the corner of her vision saw only the swing of the black cassock and the polished black rounded-toe shoes, each tied tightly with a double bow.

Romance had heard it from inside, so she was not surprised to be greeted by the rain as she made her way out. And the calendar had called for it. Leaning forward, the preacher's arm stretched like a barrier, his teeth bold in a face of concealed menace, beneath a religious smile with possible godly retribution, ensuring every hand was securely grasped and firmly shaken; letting none escape with merely a pious nod. Had it not been for the warmth she felt for the place, she might well have moved her allegiance to the church on the other side of town, favoured by the influential, black and white, good and bad, lone men, those of charity and those she believed were beyond redemption. A more hardened belief was preached and expected under that roof. And the collection plate demanded more.

Umbrellas, predominately black but some brightly coloured with golfing and soft drink advertisements, clustered before her. It was the second week into the rainy season. During the first, people would forget or trust their luck; now, no one ventured out without the appropriate protection. Later in the season the winds would strengthen considerably, and all but the strongest frames would be reversed. Romance stood back, waiting for the crowd to disperse and the black cloth clouds to part. Her height made it difficult to raise her own shabby blue octagonal device, until she could identify a space above her head, and take advantage of it.

'Would you like to come back and have lunch with me, Romance?' The preacher had taken the opportunity once all the hand-shaking was complete, and was now standing a little too close to Romance for her contentment. It was not the first time he had approached her in this manner. When he was new to the area, she had previously accepted his invitation as an offer of welcoming generosity, but then had been horrified when he attempted to press his affections as well as his food upon her. She had told the preacher then that she was a married lady, and that her husband would be most violent if she told him of the advance.

'Just lunch, Romance. It will not be like last time, I promise you that. And by then, the rain might be over. Look, there are cloud breaks with clear blue not too far off.'

She declined, offering the lie of a pre-existing invitation.

'Thank you,' she said politely, 'for the service.' Then she moved quickly away into a space that had opened.

A loud crash in the heavens made her jump, as she was navigating a narrow point in the water starting to swell and fill the gutter. A bright flash followed and the firmament opened, turning light rain once again into almost solid sheets of water. A small boy wearing new shoes jumped into a puddle and was rewarded with a clout around the head from his father, who failed to acknowledge the glee in his son's eyes. Maybe the preacher was being genuine; she wondered, should she have accepted his offer. Even with the umbrella held low she would be soaked before reaching the other side of the street. At that moment, a bakkie swung into the gutter stream and braked sharply, almost showering her legs with a low arc of muddy spray. She jumped back quickly in reflex, bumping the people behind. Her apology, given red-faced, was rewarded with a disapproving glare.

'God be with you,' she muttered, slightly below her breath, with more sarcasm than Christian goodwill.

She recognized the truck immediately and its driver, Kingsley, bookkeeper at the swimming pool supplies company where she worked; a nice young man, she felt. Shortly after she had been given the job, he had become a Muslim and changed his name, but everyone at the office still used 'Kingsley' and this did not seem to bother him. He waved her to open the door and accept a lift.

A few minutes later she was dropped outside the ironmonger's shop, a two-storey building, locked and shuttered, where she rented a single room at the rear. The street was empty, except for a striding man with his suit trousers rolled a foot up his legs and an orange box held low over his head. When necessary he danced a jig around the pools of water or harsh stones, reminding her of a child playing hopscotch.

Inside, stripped to her underwear, she had slipped into a yellow print nylon housecoat and hung her suit on a wire hanger to dry and allow the creases, caused by what she saw as her expanding body, to fall out. She hated the rainy season; it meant cooking most of the time inside her room, the smell permeating her small range of clothing. Mostly she would eat sadza with a little relish, only the hot brown gravy making the porridge meal palatable. In the dry season the owner of the store, an insular man of Asian origin who lived quietly on the second floor, did not object to her cooking on a wood-fired stove in the yard. So then, she would be able to buy kapenta from the market. For now, it was not an option as she would always be worried her work clothes reeked of the dried fish, the worst of all cooking smells to her mind.

Heavy-handed knocking on the door stopped her abruptly. She was not expecting anyone, and the thunderstorm was still not giving way to the blue sky the preacher had identified earlier. The people she knew, unless their cause was urgent or their work demanded, would rarely venture out on foot for pleasure while the rain persisted. Few owned cars. She had no thought of who it could be, and pulled the housecoat tightly around her as she opened the door sufficiently to see out. The afternoon was dark, overcast with cloud. She dipped her head as the wind, which had now picked up, flicked her face with spray from the torrent that cascaded the overflowing gutter. She could not make out who was standing before her. And, as the figure barged in past her, she was none the wiser: a sheet of black plastic wrapped around from head to foot, and a peaked cap pulled down, shielding the face completely, blanked out any possible recognition. Her apprehension turned immediately to fear. She considered running out into the rain. But there was nowhere to go, and it was unlikely there would be anyone on the street, even if she could clear the yard before being grabbed and pulled back. She knew, Sunday afternoon, her landlord slept a deadly slumber, clawing back hours lost to weekday early mornings and late nights.

'Good welcome for a drowning man who has travelled in this weather to deliver you a letter.'

The voice was irritable, that of a man who considered himself hard done by. Hearing it, she recognized her husband's brother, also the husband of her younger sister. He worked as a guard for the South African train company, and if he was on the run north, crossing the border, he would bring news from her sister in Jo'burg.

'I do not know why you live like this woman, you have a good job,' he looked around the place with disapproval as he spoke. The plastic that had protected him from the weather had been allowed to fall to the floor, creating narrow rivulets and forming a pool on the bare floor with the water squelching from his shoes. Seeing what he wanted, he crossed the small room in one stride. He picked up a towel worn thin with use, hanging beside the chipped sink, and used it to wipe the rain from his face.

Romance disliked Sonkwe and could not understand why her sister had gone off with him.

'You know why. We're saving up to buy our own house. Last year, we bought a new car,' she proudly declared.

'It wasn't new,' Sonkwe retorted.

'New to us,' she replied firmly, the pleasure still evident in her voice.

'By the time you have saved enough to start building, my brother will have wrecked it and killed himself, the way he drives. On that plot it won't be a new house, it'll be a narrow house.'

His face bore no resemblance to that of her husband. She ignored his jibes, his smirk filled with condemnation, and she bent down to pick up the plastic sheet before the room became flooded. She made an attempt to prop it in her plastic washing-up bowl. At the same time, her housecoat fell open. She did not miss Sonkwe's eyes considering her lapse of modesty. Discreetly, she turned away and pulled the thin material tight around herself once more.

'You have a letter from my sister?' she asked, freezing out the lechery she could see in his expression.

'Are you going to thank me this time for bringing it so far, and running all this way from the station with the heavens open?'

'You have not delivered it yet.' Was there an unintended hint of promise in her voice, she wondered. She hoped not.

From the inside pocket of his tailored brown cotton uniform jacket with embossed gold buttons and braid, Sonkwe removed an envelope creased at the corners, and bent to the shape of his chest. He held it out for Romance to step forward and take.

As she went to take the offering, she knew he would grab her arm. What was in his mind was in his eyes, and she knew he wanted her. She snatched quickly, but even so was not quick enough to prevent his hand closing around her wrist, pinching the skin and pulling her to him. Again her housecoat parted, exposing undergarments and flesh. She felt him against her, and a hint of his arousal.

'What will Prudence think of you treating her sister like this?' She spat the words at him, guessing the aggression in her voice did not mask the fear.

'She does what she is told, and so should you,' Sonkwe's voice was matter-of-fact; no anger, no passion. Devoid of tempo.

He did not push her onto the iron-framed bed as she thought he would, but neither did he loosen his hold, which was hurting now. She had caught him looking at her on previous occasions, but he had never made a move before. When he pulled her almost off her feet and made to kiss her, she turned her mouth away before their lips touched. There was a faint smell of alcohol on his breath, but she knew he wasn't drunk.

'I'll tell Kunda. You might be his big brother, but he'll kill you, you touch me,' she shouted, her voice deepening, still keeping her face turned away. Slowly she felt his hold slacken; he dropped her and stepped back. In her mind she saw her husband standing next to his brother. Kunda was half a head shorter, and forty pounds lighter, but he had a focus about him that his elder brother had never displayed. She knew they were close; she also knew Sonkwe was scared of the smaller man. Something in the past, but she did not know what, and she had never asked.

'The way he drive, he be dead before long. Then you have no choice,' he dropped the envelope, which she had failed to grasp, on the floor. Taking his plastic sheet, he walked out of the door, into the storm, without saying another word.

oOo

Kingsley's desk was adjacent to the glass-fronted manager's office. Romance walked slowly across the office to it, carrying two cups of coffee, each with two chocolate-chip biscuits balanced in the saucers. Although not required to make the coffee, she undertook this task out of choice. And she had decided to thank Kingsley for the lift the previous day, with biscuits from her personal supply. Not feeling she could exclude her boss, she had also added the sweet snack to his standard request 'milky without sugar', even though it would mean purchasing a new packet before the end of the week.

Romance worked for a business that was doing well. More private homes were installing pools, and the hotels and lodges were all reporting good occupancy. Kingsley worked harder than ever, which was reflected by the stacks of invoices and delivery notes arranged across his desk, so much so it was difficult for Romance to set down his coffee without disturbing one pile or another. Kingsley looked up, smiled his soft genial smile, and took the welcome beverage from her. Mr Simons was not in his office, but she knew he would be back from the yard shortly. She left the cup on his side-table, hoping the heat would not melt the chocolate before he returned.

Mr Simons was not the owner; he had arrived from England to work as Mr Robertson's assistant on 14th June 1999, the same day Thabo Mbeki became President down south. Within a few months, the enthusiastic young Englishman had taken over the reins. Mr Robertson had visited the UK to celebrate the coming of the new millennium with his family, and had been persuaded to remain. He returned once, but only for a couple weeks, and left when he had assured himself all was running in accordance with his expectations. Mr Simons was young, not much older than Romance herself, with ginger hair and a face full of freckles which became almost solid orange when he spent more than a little time in the sun. He seemed more relaxed, spoke to her with respect, and did not get angry in the way Mr Robertson had, when things did not go exactly right.

Romance's job was to prepare the worksheets for the clients who had requested their pool to be cleaned, which was normally only done at private houses, and to arrange the supply of chemicals on a regular basis to the other clients. Keeping the pools clean was very important, Mr Robertson had explained on her first day: 'Miss a clean or let it go too long, and swimmers could catch bilharzia and die.' Romance thought he was being ridiculous. She had never heard of anyone dying from dirty, infested swimming pools. There were stagnant ponds near the river that displayed warning signs, and she had heard of people being paralysed by the microscopic worms carried by freshwater snails, but a swimming pool missing a clean… She had decided it was just a Robertson sales gimmick. She was not stupid.

Most of the bulk stock used by the company was delivered to the yard by truck from Jo'burg, but on regular occasions items were missing completely or delivered short, making it difficult to schedule the work when the client requested or contracts demanded. Mr Simons had changed the carrier shortly after taking over, and this had reduced the losses and made her job much easier.

Kunda, Romance's husband, had worked out that in another four years Romance could give up her job and return to the village. They would be able to build their own house on a good-sized plot, out on the main road, close to the church. Kunda had been an enthusiastic happy-clapper, which Romance understood matched his fun-loving personality, and was one of the reasons she loved him so much. More recently she thought his attendance must have waned, due to the long hours he spent at work. Whenever she heard from him it was work, work, work.

Though she remembered it had originally been three years, Kunda told her land prices were increasing, so by the time they had saved sufficient, the cost would be a little more than they had budgeted. Romance was lucky: to ensure loyalty Mr Robertson had arranged to pay all his staff in US dollars rather than the local currency. Kunda was not so fortunate in that aspect, but he did get tips in a variety of valuable foreign currencies. Chocolate-chip cookies were one of the very few luxuries Romance permitted for herself: everything else went into the pot for their future.

Walking home at the end of the day, she had intended to stop at the supermarket. But the rain had started again, so she changed her mind. It was at times like this she wished Kunda had let the car remain with her. The roads were better in town, and there was less chance of the tyres getting torn. But he was right, she knew, as she only had a few blocks to walk to work, and he could earn extra money giving lifts to the gardeners, waiters and chefs. Still, she was worried the village roads, always badly maintained and full of holes, could cause damage. Tyres, even secondhand tyres, were expensive. And, as Sonkwe had said, Kunda was not a careful driver. By the time she reached her room, the rain had proved only to be a shower, and the concrete in the yard was again dry and dusty. With the coming of the rains, grass and weeds were beginning to sprout through the cracks. She decided she could plant out her boxes with vegetable seeds next weekend. Rocket, courgettes and potatoes would soon provide a welcome change to her staple diet of the past months, and give her the opportunity to vary her cooking skills. The rainy season had some positive aspects.

Weeks passed and little changed. At work, some of the contracts had been suspended as lodges closed for the rainy season and pools were drained. Before they were refilled, she would arrange for crews to go in and scrub them out with neat chemicals, repaint and if necessary replace broken tiles. But that would not be for months. The stacks of invoices on Kingsley's desk grew smaller, and at the end of November Mr Simons travelled to South Africa to visit old suppliers and meet with their competitors. Then, after being back only a few days, he left again to explore the possibilities of opening an office, or appointing an agent, in the far north of the country, which enjoyed little in the way of tourist hotels but had prospered extensively from mining wealth. In the office, they had expected him to be back from his last trip within a week, but he did not return for more than two. No one could decide whether this was a good sign, or if he had needed the extra days because there had been little interest. Mr Simons did not elaborate, although Kingsley thought his mood was darker when he did eventually return.

With the coming of the heavier rains, the congregation at church had thinned. From early in December, Romance had noticed that the tall lean woman who, for at least the past year without fail, had always stood to her right, was not in evidence. As far as Romance could see, her usual position unoccupied, she did not appear to be in any other seat. Little else had changed at the Sunday service. The preacher still shook Romance's hand warmly, as he did with the rest of his flock each week, but made no further advances in the way of dubious invitations. The season powered up with deluges of rain and storm-force winds, which lashed the water in swirls down the street and was not beyond throwing open the heavy wooden church doors in the middle of prayer or sermon.

'The Lord cometh,' the preacher would reply, with equal

gusto; the youths in the back row springing up to close the door and slide the heavy metal bolt.

At night, Romance curled up, protected under her mosquito net, watching fuzzy TV, and sometimes re-reading her sister's letter, pondering the contents. She had considered taking some days off to make a visit, then volunteering to man the office over Christmas to make up the time. Not that there would be any calls during the holiday, but the stock was valuable and Mr Robertson had always insisted the premises should not be left unattended for too long. She knew Kunda expected her to go to the village, and would be angry if she worked at Christmas for no extra money. She thought, hoped, Sonkwe might deliver another letter, as Prudence had promised to write again soon. Either he had been on the Cape Town line running to the south, or had chosen not to put himself out again, after their last encounter.

oOo

'Do you know where you are going?' The youthful inspector demanded.

'The next turning on the left, I think,' the driver answered, nervous that his uncertainty would bring rebuke.

He was driving an officer, a detective in fact, who had flown in from the capital the same morning, appearing to have left behind any tolerance he might have cultivated at the check-in desk.

'It's the second on the left.' The sergeant sitting behind them leaned forward. 'I was passed there a few days ago.'

'How come you don't know where anything is round here? The place is no bigger than a piss-pot.'

The driver ignored the remark for fear of further annoying the senior officer, whatever his reply.

'They have changed a lot of the street names recently. Nobody is sure where anywhere is any more,' the sergeant said, pointing to a painted-out nameplate that had not yet been replaced on the side wall of a fried chicken takeaway.

The inspector took a well-worn green folder, with previous case names scratched out, from the dashboard and flicked through the slim contents to refresh his appreciation of the significant facts; not that these were normally reflected in his approach to criminal matters.

'When we get there, you stay at the front door,' the inspector told the driver. 'Sergeant, you come in with me. Keep your eyes open, I don't want the suspect slipping away. If he tries to run for it, and you value your skin, make sure you don't stand in my line of fire.'

Two uniformed police, and a slim young man in a smart suit, stopped outside the office. Romance had seen them pull up and get out. The suited one adjusted his dark glasses, raised his chin to view the sign above the office door, and then barged in, almost taking the door off its hinges.

'Bless the Lord' Romance exclaimed as the door smashed against her desk.

'Where's your boss?'

'England,' she answered as abruptly.

Romance did not like being treated in this manner, and could be as uncivil as the next person, despite her natural tendency to quiet good manners.

'Not him, the other one.'

'Not here.'

'Hiding out the back won't do him any good,' the inspector told her, 'and if you help him get away I'll take you as well.'

'He is not out the back and I am not going to be taken away by you or anyone else. He's out the front trying to come in, but your officer out there is barring his way,' she informed her adversary in a tone that did not disguise the comedy unfolding before them.

Moments later, the double-cab Land Rover sped away

with Mr Simons sitting cuffed in the rear cage. Kids in smart school uniforms settled on the small veranda outside the takeaway, eating chips from card cones or licking ice-pops, shouted their disapproval as street dirt from the tyres dusted them and their snacks.

Romance did not know what she should be doing. All of the crews were out on deliveries and Kingsley, sitting at the far end of the office, had not said a word or shown any sign of emotion throughout the whole short incident. He had remained his constant, quiet, composed self. Romance did not know what to say; she thought for a moment and then decided she should make Kingsley and herself a cup of tea.

When she returned with the two cups, she also brought with her an almost full packet of biscuits. It had been unopened, but while waiting for the kettle to boil she had indulged more than once. The extraordinary events of a few minutes ago without question provided justification, she felt sure. She found Kingsley sitting in Mr Simons' office, just replacing the phone handset.

CHAPTER TWO

The youthful inspector had not liked being made to look foolish, and his treatment of Stephen Simons reflected his irritation. Although most things irritated him and his treatment of prisoners, both black and white, was never known to be anything but ruthless. The red rings around Stephen's wrists were raw where the cuffs had been hooked a few inches higher than would allow his body weight to be absorbed by the bench seat in the back of the wagon. The journey to the police station had taken less than ten minutes, but the time had been sufficient to draw blood and cause him pain.

He had never been in the building before, but had passed by on many occasions when handling the company banking. The moment he entered, he knew it was a place that did not recognize the normal elements of common decency. Lino floors, walls half-tiled with a dark green marble effect, the top half painted in a matching shade, which had begun to peel years earlier, and a ceiling now thickly coated with the tar of a million cigarettes. Pools of light, from unshaded low-wattage bulbs, added to the feeling of neglect and despair. A scream echoing along one of the corridors went without acknowledgement, neither from the few police officers hanging around, nor from any of the badly composed human assortment arranged on benches against the wall, waiting. Waiting for their turn. Stephen shuddered. This was only the reception area and he knew, like the omnipresent odour of urine and vomit, it would get worse the deeper one ventured. He did not imagine he had been picked up and treated in this manner purely on a visa violation.

'I am in charge of this investigation. You will do as I tell you and no harm will come to you. You will be dealt with, and your punishment will be decided by the courts. The sergeant will write down what we know and you will sign it,' The inspector informed him within minutes of being taken to an interview room, a box that closely resembled the reception in colour and ambience. A small dark wooden table, gouged, burnt and stained with blood or coffee, probably both, and two bare-wood chairs, stood in the centre.

The sergeant was sat across the table from Stephen, leaning over a blank sheet of paper, holding a worn-down pencil between tight fingers, ready to transcribe his confession.

Stephen turned to look at the inspector, who was now standing behind him. But before Stephen could bring him into view, the man had landed an open palm around his head. Not hard, but with enough power to rock him in his chair.

'You do only what I tell you, hear?'

Stephen had expected to be taken to the reception desk, when he arrived at the station, and to be told what was going on. He had still not been given any indication as to why he was here. His brain was working sufficiently well to realize he was probably in a state of shock.

'Sir, can you please tell me why I am here, because whatever the reason I am sure there has been some mistake,' Stephen spoke slowly, keeping his breathing steady, in the hope the fear that was a freezing block in the pit of his stomach would not be evident.

'You speak when I tell you, hear?' The words were accompanied by a second slap. 'There is no mistake, except your mistake.'

'What do you think the mistake I have made is?' Stephen retorted, without really thinking.

Stephen did not hear any answer. The sound of his chair clattering on the ground, the loud ringing in his right ear and the echo in his head as it hit the floor, blocked out all other sound. The inspector had not offered a reply, and the slap this time had been more than cursory.

The sergeant came round the table; Stephen could feel the man's bony fingers pinch into his flesh as he hauled him back upright and into the chair. The inspector came from behind and squarely pushed the statement across the table in front of him, holding out a gold pen. Stephen's eyes focused before the ringing in his ears had subsided. The nails on this man's hand were filed and polished, the quick neatly manicured. The fingers, without jewellery; the arms leading up to a lean, but not skinny, torso. It was the first time he had really looked at the man who was now abusing him. The suit could have been handmade outside Africa and the face, he felt sure, must have been covered with a mask. No one with such a sadistic mind could own the smooth, clear, creamy, ebony, cherubic face that was now less than a foot from his own.

'Sign.'

'Sign what?'

'Your statement.'

'It's blank.'

'Just sign, the sergeant will fill in the details.'

The sergeant looked only slightly less amused than Stephen at the prospect.

'That's not how we normally do things down here.'

The inspector gave the sergeant a glance in reply to the comment. Stephen would not have been surprised had it been accompanied by a slap similar to the one he had received. The sergeant had made his stand, but did not seem willing to go further. Stephen retained sufficient clarity to realize that even if the statement was written, it would be in pencil, changeable. His signature in ink, irrefutable.

When Stephen failed to show any sign of taking the pen still being offered, the inspector's foot lunged forward onto the frame of the chair, sending it and Stephen back to the floor. The sergeant remained seated.

'Sign or don't, the courts will still find you guilty. And in this country, we still have the death penalty. Better you plead guilty and ask the court for mercy. It is the only way you have a chance that the judge will not put on his black cap.'

The heat of Stephen's anger did not melt the block of ice cramping his stomach.

'Guilty of what? What is it I'm supposed to have done?' Stephen remained lying on the concrete, making no attempt to get up.

'You visited the villa of Mr Fumina during the first few days of this month? And don't lie; we have witnesses.'

At last. The accusation. The mistake. The way out.

'Why should I lie? This is ridiculous. He is one of our clients,' Stephen muttered with a momentary flicker of hope in his voice.

'So you admit it.' The inspector snatched at the reply with a sense of triumph as if it were a physical object. 'Sergeant, write that down. It is an admission of guilt.'

Stephen began to get up; he felt at last he was beginning to get somewhere, despite the tunnel vision of his interrogator. If he could find out what he was being accused of exactly, he felt sure it would not take too long to prove all this was a ridiculous mistake.

'Yes, I admit going to his house. Mr Fumina is in Maputo; he spends many months there on business and is not likely to be back until the new year. He left at the beginning of November, and I sent a team in to drain and clean his pool, as he asked. I was travelling north, and on my way I called in to ensure a good job had been done.'

'But you didn't just look at the pool did you, you went into the house, and we can prove it. You broke in…'

'Why would I break in? We hold a key, so that we can turn off the alarm to the plant room. The pumps and filter system are expensive. Mr Fumina has it alarmed. I went in the back door, turned off the alarm, checked everything out and locked up before I left.'

'Mr Simons, every time you open your mouth, you admit more. Sergeant, did you get that?' The inspector said from behind a broadening smile.

The sergeant nodded and wrote a short sentence on the sheet of paper that was now beginning to fill with his small, tight scribble.

'Mr Simons, you went there knowing Mr Fumina was in Mozambique and would not be back for many weeks. You went there, not to check if the work he had ordered had been carried out correctly, but for your own evil purposes. You let yourself in, turned off the alarm and, during the next number of hours, committed your evil deed, smashing a window to make it look like a break-in as you left. But, in the panic of what you had done, you forgot to turn the alarm back on.'

The ice turned to freezing water, and ran through every vein in his body as he tried to remember putting the key back into the panel and pressing the reset button. He knew sweat had broken out across his forehead. He felt he had to say something.

'I touched nothing and there was nobody there. It was all as it should be and that was the way I left it.'

'You have turned very pale, Mr Simons. Sergeant, get

the prisoner a glass of water, before we go to search his accommodation.'

Stephen Simons lived in a small rented villa along the airport road, on the edge of town. The police had spent an hour turning each room upside down without finding anything, as far as Stephen could tell, that was at all incriminating. Throughout, he had remained handcuffed and standing. Now they had moved their attention to the thousand square metres of garden. Stephen did not think even the most thorough search could take long as the area consisted almost entirely of finely mown grass, with the exception of a very clean pool. Unless, of course, they were going to start digging. But with what objective, he could not imagine. Stolen goods? Stephen considered the likelihood. But surely, he tried to rationalize, stealing didn't carry the death penalty, not even here.

The sergeant left the area where he was poking about, and returned to the Land Rover. He was responding to a small red bulb flashing on the dashboard, which obviously had some significance. He walked round to the driver's side and was blocked from Stephen's view by one of the large concrete gate pillars and a bougainvillea. Moments later he came back and spoke quietly to the inspector from behind a cupped hand, discreetly enough for Stephen not to even pick out the odd word or make an untrained attempt at lip-reading.

'Call for another vehicle to come and collect you. I will take the Land Rover and him.' The inspector spoke with a note of impatience and nodded towards Stephen.

An hour passed and they had driven without stopping, Stephen again manacled in the cage. Within minutes of beginning the journey, to wherever, the sky had opened and the rain had not shown any sign of moderating. The weather appeared to be clearing from the south, but in heading north they seemed to be on the same path as the black clouds. Stephen saw the analogy in this, and hoped it

21

was not an omen. He had recognized the road as that on which he had driven earlier in the month, long before they sped past Mr Fumina's home. Although passing at speed, and the low level house being set back from the road on a short, well-groomed drive, as far as Stephen could make out there was no indication of activity on the property.

For another hour they journeyed over good roads that lapsed from time to time into long stretches of dereliction. The Land Rover swerved often to miss potholes, and areas bitten out from the edge by baking heat and persistent rain; a tribute not to this season, but rather to years of government neglect. Stephen was only prevented from being thrown from one side of the cage to another by the shackles anchoring him in position, hands aloft. Blood soaked the cuffs of his jacket and congealed in stalactites that vibrated, as did everything, with the mechanics of the vehicle. Stephen was close to passing out when, finally, the Land Rover came to an abrupt stop. Outside, he could see the busy industry of a small town and its community. Billboards lined the road, advertising everything from cars to condoms. People looked in at him as they walked by. Whites caged in the rear of police vehicles were obviously a curiosity. The inspector climbed out of the cab, slamming the door closed behind him.

'You give me money, I will buy you food,' he said, taking the keys to the cage from his pocket ready to open up. Stephen remained silent, not knowing if he were capable of swallowing food, even if he were permitted to eat.

The decision was taken away from him, as the inspector leaned in and removed the wallet from inside Stephen's jacket, took out the notes, and pushed the black leather pouch back, then locked up and left. A moment later, he returned.

'You escape, I will shoot you.' As he spoke, he opened his jacket to display a short-barrelled revolver in a holster clipped to his belt. 'That might be best with what you have got to look forward to, but I will leave your bones for the vultures. At least where you are heading, you will get a funeral of sorts. So, remember that.'

Stephen did not believe in any afterlife, but he had seen vultures strutting around road-kill on his travels about the country, and the thought was not a good one. His flesh being torn from the bone, even after death had taken all knowledge and feeling, did not appeal. He was not capable of engaging his brain to look beyond the now. How he might effect this escape, he could not figure.

He thought he must have passed out, because it seemed his captor had once again returned immediately after leaving for a second time, but he was laden with greaseproof-paper-wrapped sandwiches and two bottles of water. The inspector looked at him hard. Stephen decided he was making sure his prisoner had not found some Houdini magic that would allow him to spring from the cab the moment the gate was unlocked.

Without speaking, his captor walked back round to the cab and a few moments later the engine was gunned. The journey had restarted. Stephen had purchased the food and drink, but had not been a recipient of either. Silently he mouthed swear words he rarely used.

Another hour passed and Stephen, falling in and out of consciousness, noticed they were entering another small town which appeared impossible to distinguish from the previous. Computers and condoms drifted in and out of focus.

Half-conscious haze or dust-clouded view, whether it was the same town or another, or whether he was back in the first police station where this nightmare had started, he did not know. It looked the same, the smell was reminiscent, but he guessed they conformed to a standard structure throughout the country, and their usage identical.

Again, he found himself sitting in a chair in a bare room

with the inspector shouting at him. Not angry, just loud. Stephen felt appalling. Glancing down at himself, he saw a man who could have just stumbled into habitation from days trekking across the desert; a survivor of some unreported disaster. To Stephen's eye, the inspector looked no different from when he had walked into Stephen's life an unknown number of hours earlier. What appeared to be the same statement sheet lay on a table that appeared to be the same table, or a very close relation.

He wanted to tell the inspector that he did not know the answer to any of the questions, if in fact they were questions; maybe they were commands. Either way, he could not respond. His throat was closed, parched, and his tongue felt as though it had swollen to fill the whole of his mouth: an emergency air bag inflated in a confined space. His arms and shoulders were heavy as lead. He pictured himself in some early Kirk Douglas religious epic carrying building rubble on a heavy wooden yoke. He could not contemplate why these ridiculous images were beginning to fill his mind. He would have laughed, had he the ability.

When he came to, he struggled with his disoriented thoughts to identify his location. But as his eyes began to focus, it all started to become regretfully familiar. The inspector was now in shirt sleeves, standing at a strange angle. Becoming more aware, he realized he was lying in a pool of water. He pushed his tongue from his mouth, without considering the possibility that it was his own urine – worse still, that of a police officer or previous unfortunate. He licked around his lips. It was his first liquid since before he had been picked up by this shit. Whenever that was.

'Mr Simons, we are staying here tonight. If you sign this statement, you will be given a cell on your own. If not …' the inspector's voice trailed off, then he spoke again. 'Do not believe what the government says: HIV/AIDS is widespread in the prisons of this country.'

Stephen did not sign, and did not share a cell. No other prisoners were being held in that police station that night. There was no bed. He did not know whether this was normal or if the inspector had arranged for the bed in that cell to be removed. A bucket, still half full of the previous occupants' toilet, stood in the corner. A low-voltage dust-caked, bare bulb flickered. Still cuffed, he sat in the corner with his knees pulled up to his chest. Cold, shaking, he spent the night drifting in and out of darkness. From time to time his nostrils took in a smell that he thought could be rotting flesh. He did not know if this was the smell of gangrene – his, or from elsewhere. It was a question he asked himself. Then, he asked himself another, out loud this time, to which he did not know the answer: 'How long does it take to set in?'

Earlier on, he had torn some of his shirt and attempted to stuff it as protection between his wrists and the manacles, but that had fallen away. He tried to push macabre thoughts from his mind. Boarding school nearly two decades earlier. Sandhurst, not so long ago. Would the whole of his life be punctuated by intolerable episodes, he deliberated. He could think of no reason it should, but here it was bringing terror into his daily routine once more.

In the morning he was given a bowl of sadza and a tin mug of cold water. A uniformed policeman bandaged his wrists the best he could, using strips of dirty rag. He was shackled in the back of the Land Rover again, and a new journey began. The sun was shining. Blood had already succeeded in turning the grey wristbands red. He drifted into what seemed to be the original police station, then uncountable cells identical to the first he had slept in. Images came and went without him being able to anchor himself in any: headmaster pushing his hand level with the stick, before administering the cane ... woman shouting and swearing at him when he could not service her needs ... sergeant major, cap peak steamed to his nose, flogging him in full kit round the track. Crying, crying, crying. Condoms and hair-straightening products. He prayed for rain.

After the sun was high, he began to notice scatterings of tin shacks on either side of the road, which became increasingly dense. He had never travelled by road into the capital, always flying in, but he was aware of a large shanty town on the outskirts, housing tens of thousands of refugees from Zaire. It was this group that bore the brunt of blame for most of the violent crime that plagued the city. He guessed they were on the outskirts of the capital – no other area in southern Africa had this accumulation, as far as he was aware, except Soweto in South Africa. But he was sure, even with long periods of blacking out, there was no way they had travelled that kind of distance. And why?

Slowly the ramshackle, junk-constructed shelters teeming with the dispossessed, and skeleton dogs scavenging the remains of the remains, gave way to the formal construction of residential dwellings, office blocks and small retail stores, fast food outlets feeding the fat cats, and billboards selling the same cars, computers and condoms.

Stephen tumbled, as he was piloted between a line of parked police cars, towards the entrance of the city's main police station.

'You will be charged, and held in prison until your case can be heard,' the inspector told him, as he grabbed Stephen's shoulder and pushed him through the double doors into the busy reception area.

'Mr Simons? Stephen Simons?' A well-spoken voice seemed to be booming his name.

Stephen did not respond; certain nobody here would be calling him, and his head was spinning.

'Inspector Kashula, if I'm not mistaken?' The inspector stopped and pulled Stephen to a standstill. Turning, he saw a large, well-dressed Indian-looking chap with white hair, striding in their direction. Stephen noticed a look of what appeared to be disgust cross the inspector's face.

'You have my client there, I believe,' he said, addressing the inspector, and then turning to Stephen, added, 'Johal. Of Cron Johal Solicitors. I'm representing you and, if the inspector here can find us a room, we'll have a quick chat. See if we can't get this matter sorted out.'

'Sanjay Johal,' the solicitor said gently. 'Had a bit of a song and dance trying to find you.'

Stephen was sitting once again at a small wooden table in a room almost identical to the numerous rooms he had occupied over however long it was since he had been apprehended outside his office. The only difference this time was that the officer, Inspector Kashula, was not in the room intimidating him.

'It is not unusual for suspects to be moved around the country to prevent people like me poking my nose in. Now tell me, did you sign anything?' Johal asked.

'I don't think so,' Stephen replied thoughtfully, trying to recall every moment and the pressures he had been put under. He knew, given the opportunity, his mind would reject as much of the nightmare as it could, but he was as sure as he could be. The abuses during his school days, and then later, were masked. The brain had a way of blocking out the unbearable.

'Good. And have you been formally charged?' Johal's voice sounded upbeat, but Stephen thought this was just a ploy Johal maintained to keep his clients from falling into depths of despair.

'Truthfully, I'm not sure. It's all a bit hazy.'

'Well, at least you are still alive. Inspector Kashula has an unsavoury reputation. If he does not shoot someone every week, he gets really irritable.' Johal grinned. 'Now, if you'll excuse me, I will go and find out what's happening. I only arrived here a few minutes before you, I'm afraid,' he added, getting up. 'We couldn't locate you, so finally I decided to fly up here. My guess was, with the seriousness of the accusation, this is where you would end up. If you had been charged already, I think you would have been taken straight to the prison, so this all looks very encouraging.'

'I didn't do it,' Stephen blurted out, not sure what it was exactly he was denying.

'I'm sure,' Johal said, and he and the smile were gone.

CHAPTER THREE

Rumour had been rife everywhere Romance went on Saturday morning, in the shops and around the stalls in the market, where she had gone to buy dried mopani. Even Romance's landlord had accosted her, as she returned home, to ask the question. Mr Fumina's sister had apparently been found, hacked to death, at his house. Romance had been unaware that he had a sister, or even a sister-in-law, and certainly any time she had telephoned to arrange a crew visit, there had never been a woman answering the call. As far as she knew Mr Fumina was not even married. Gossip was the opiate of the uneducated, she had once heard someone say. It may have been the preacher that had now gone away. Certainly the speculation was horrible, but much of the detail was consistent enough to make it plausible.

At church on Sunday, the preacher had not waited to waylay her at the end of the service: he was at the main entrance looking out for her when she arrived. Immediately his large hand pulled her to one side, away from the other members of the arriving congregation, twizzling their umbrellas and heading in to escape the weather. She looked up into his flat, round face, never having noticed previously the odd, deep indent in his left temple, even when he had been so close that she could taste the fumes from the liquor consumed with the meal he had served: liquor she had refused, in the face of his determined hospitality.

'Romance my dear, I understand your boss, the white manager at your office, has been arrested and charged with the brutal murder of the young woman who stood with you here in my church each week. Killing one of my flock.' Each time he used *my*, Romance could not help but notice his emphasis on the word.

Three people, none of whom she really knew, but whose lives brushed hers in close proximity on occasion: she was still sceptical that the rumours involving all three could be true. Certainly, the tall lean woman who had stood mouthing hymns next to her for a year or more had suddenly disappeared from the ranks of worshippers. Certainly, Mr Simons had been abruptly taken from the office by police, in a very frightening manner. And it seemed without question, a dead woman had been found at the house of Mr Fumina, a man she knew to be extremely polite in all their telephone conversations. All seemingly nice people. All being spoken of in gossip regarding a wholly vile act.

Romance missed church that day. Instead of continuing inside with the preacher, she had turned away and hurried back to her room, where she sat quietly. Later, privately, she prayed.

Finding it difficult to marshal her thoughts, she felt in no position to form an opinion. Whatever the truth, and the truth she believed would rise above the street tittle-tattle, it was upsetting. Staring into the mirror, she examined herself. The word *my* had made her angry, it had somehow repelled her.

'If I belong to anyone,' she spoke out loud, 'it is to God, this country and my husband. Not some dent-faced, lecherous preacher.'

The moment the description of the man of God had flowed from her mouth, she felt ashamed. But, she still found it difficult to repress the hint of a smile that had crept into her reflection.

If she had insurance cover, she would have taken one of the trucks that afternoon and driven out to Mr Fumina's house, in an effort to establish if any of what she had heard could be true. She had learned to drive in the car she and Kunda had purchased. Her husband had been reluctant: the cost was not insignificant. But what was the point in owning a vehicle and not being able to drive? She felt that driving a bakkie could not be too different from a car. As it was, she re-read her sister's letter, and tried to picture the woman she had only really ever seen from the corner of her vision, and wondered who would mourn if something dreadful also happened to herself. Was isolation common amongst women everywhere, she reflected, not having considered this before. Men had friends. Men congregated in groups, drank together and played games. Women were possessions, they worked, they had children, they nattered to each other at standpipes, over the counter and doing the laundry. But when she had left the village, it was only her husband who had ever written. Who were the dead woman's friends, she speculated. Was she missed?

Preparing dinner, she strained the water-soaked mopani worms in the chinois and fried them in a shallow pan until they were crispy, then added some tomato sauce and chilli powder to enhance the flavour. A puff of steam settled on her face as she poured boiling water over the seasoned sadza. Stirring a smaller amount than usual, she was ever hopeful of losing a little weight before seeing Kunda. She missed her husband and did not want him to think she had got fat since they were last together. Eating with her fingers, she scooped up the thick, white paste, moulded it into a ball, and dipped it into the relish. Not wanting to contaminate it with food, she turned the pages of her sister's letter with the other hand.

She could not recall the number of times she had read and re-read the letters HIV. Millions of people throughout southern Africa were infected, but she had never thought it would take her little sister. Now that must surely be the case. Almost worse, written in a trembled hand, Prudence swore she had been faithful to Sonkwe, but he was not showing any signs of the illness. Prudence's fears were clear; if he found out about her infection he would beat her, throw her out and take a new wife.

Romance used the last of the white porridge to mop up the final drops of the liquid, creating red lines around the plate, as she contemplated how best to help her sister. She had money saved. Money could buy drugs. But her savings were for the house, and she would have to ask Kunda to part with the funds. She knew she could not stand by while Prudence wasted away, but she did not want to lose her husband because of it. Prudence was married to his brother; surely he would agree that she could spend money helping family. Surely he would understand it was the right thing to do. She was convinced, but still nervous as to how best she should approach the subject.

During the night, she awoke abruptly. The thought had not previously occurred to her, but now she was terrified the reason Sonkwe had not returned was that he had found out and done exactly what her sister had so feared. With nothing, and nowhere to go, Prudence may try to head north. Would she come here? Or, find her way back to their village? Or, would her sister languish on the streets, finding shelter in one of Jo'burg's shanty towns. She tried to prevent her thoughts going beyond that.

She lay wet with sweat, listening to the relentless roar of the lorries on their haul north, having crossed the border earlier in the day from South Africa, escaping the mayhem of the nearby customs crossing, where gangs worked the parking lots. They could steal anything and everything, from wrenched-off hubcaps and wing mirrors to cases of liquor and TV sets in quantity, jemmied from locked containers. They could provide false documents and access to bribeable officials, or simply take payment for a jump to the front of the queue before customs slammed down the shutters on the unlucky stranded hordes, and closed for the night; those worrying over lost time, others apprehensive and vulnerable. Those who had made it through, drivers paid by the load, were sleep-deprived and foot-flat towards their destination. Was Prudence with one of them? Romance wondered what they would demand in return for the ride.

Turning over, she tried to encourage sleep; pushing out thoughts and sounds, she struggled to capture any pleasant dreams. Once she thought she heard lion far off, the sound being carried across on the waters of the Zambezi. It would not be long: if the rains continued as expected, the river would be in full flow; the Smoke That Thunders would have drowned out any such possibility.

In the morning she rose early, washed, dressed and left for work, her quandary still unresolved. She knew she would be first to arrive, but she had a key and would welcome the chance to occupy her mind with easy things. While the office was quiet, it might be a good opportunity to overhaul the filing system, she mulled as she walked, oblivious to her familiar surroundings. It was bright; the rain would arrive later.

Although early, the town was already busy; only offices and the bank did not open their doors until nine. A few doors away from the office she stopped abruptly, stepping into the delivery doorway of the southern fried chicken takeaway, as she realized it was Mr Simons she was watching, unlocking the office and going in. Without really thinking, she turned and walked away in the opposite direction. She was not sure why: a question she asked herself later, but found she was still unable to answer.

By the time she had finished her machine-dispensed coffee, an hour had slipped away. As she sat in the snack area of the main street petrol station, the confusion of her thoughts had eaten up her time: flashes of her sister, her brother-in-law, Mr Simons, the woman missing from the church bench next to her, the few extra pounds she had put on that she hoped Kunda would not notice. Confident other members of staff would be in the yard, or floating around the office, Romance tossed her cardboard cup in the bin and headed back. The filing reorganization would have to wait for another day.

Mr Simons had everyone assembled around the office when she walked in. Last, it appeared, to arrive.

'Romance, please find a seat. I would like to talk to everyone,' Mr Simons solemnly said, lifting his head and meeting Romance's eyes. She immediately sat in one of the soft chairs reserved for the few clients who called into the office from time to time. Everyone was somewhat apprehensive at the message they were all about to be given. She could not afford to lose her job, but feared the worst. Looking around at the other faces, she found it difficult to evaluate the mood. All would, she knew, also fear for their jobs. Sad, worried, angry. None of the eighteen faces held a positive expression. The message could surely not be good.

Mr Simons stretched to his full height to address his audience. As he did so, the long sleeves of his white shirt lifted off his wrists, exposing neat bandaging. Romance wondered if the wounds they covered were self-inflicted. But most of all, she wondered how the man, rumoured to have hacked a woman to death in the home of one of their customers, was now able to stand free before them. Not that she believed Mr Simons to be capable of such a foul deed. Money. Corruption. It was not unheard of – the police and the judges were no better than each other, but she would have expected him to have quietly boarded a plane, before awkward questions began to circulate, and certainly not to have returned to fire all the staff, before leaving.

'I would like to thank everyone here for continuing to work, in my absence. I understand that it must have been a very difficult fortnight with such unsavoury rumours that I am sure were flying around. And I would particularly like to thank Kingsley for immediately contacting Mr Robertson, who in turn instructed his solicitors. Without their legal, how shall I put it, clout, I feel I could still be languishing behind bars, and the true culprits would not have been identified.'

This statement was delivered as a burst of enthusiasm, without pondering or hardly a space given to draw breath.

'Once again, thank you for your support, and I can't tell you how glad I am to be back where I feel I somehow belong,' he added.

For a moment everyone seemed quite taken aback. The room plunged into silence when Mr Simons stopped speaking, pregnant with doubt and a little embarrassment. Romance observed the looks on each face in turn as slowly they took on expressions of relief, and smiles cracked. Then, led by Kingsley, they all broke into genuine applause.

Mr Simons grinned, having for a moment wondered if he had pitched his words somehow wrongly. 'OK, shall we all get back to work.'

Without further kerfuffle the work force dispersed.

As midday approached Romance, who had eaten more biscuits than her normal allowance, took the decision to forgo lunch and save it in the fridge until the next day. Normally, she brought in a snack each day from home, to avoid the expense and temptation of the fast-food operators – although she knew that before it was time to leave for the day, she would have to be stronger willed than she had been in the morning, where the biscuits were concerned. But this morning, she told herself, was a little out of the ordinary. She thought of Kunda and the closeness of the Christmas holiday, and decided she could muster the fortitude.

'Mr Simons has asked you and I to join him for lunch.'

Kingsley spoke in his usual soft tone, smiling pleasantly as he appeared at the entrance to the alcove that housed Romance's desk and filing cabinets, and was sometimes referred to as her office.

'You go with him, I have plenty to do. I intended to work through,' Romance replied, although without the conviction she felt she should have projected.

'Mr Simons will be disappointed. It is his way of thanking us for holding the fort,' Kingsley explained.

'You did far more than me. I just turned up as usual,' Romance protested, busying herself.

'Are we all ready then?' Mr Simons asked, arriving behind Kingsley, as he pulled on his light-coloured linen jacket.

'Who's going to look after the office?' Romance asked, in a last-ditch effort to stem her calorie intake.

Her boss proudly fluttered a sheet of paper with a handwritten message in green marker pen – *Back At 2 pm*. 'Stick it on the door, and turn the answer machine on. Come on. Let's get a move on. If our order isn't in before it fills up, we won't be back before three. Then we'd be in trouble.'

Smiling, he ushered Kingsley towards the door and handed Romance the notice. Romance folded.

The True Zoo was an informal restaurant, a short walk from the office, in a unit similar to the property in which Romance lived. The kitchen and a few tables were set up in what would have been the shop area and the bar, with the greater number of the tables situated in the unsurfaced yard out the back, shaded overhead by woven sticks. Mr Simons selected a table in the corner, and a waitress with sun-bleached braided hair, wearing cargo shorts and a True Zoo logo'd T-shirt, left them with laminated menu cards while she went to fill their drinks order.

Romance had walked past the restaurant almost every day, but had never ventured in. Even with Kunda, it would not have been a place towards which she would gravitate. It served mainly what a British newspaper had recently termed the 'new colonials': young Brits, Aussies and white South Africans, with a spattering of New Zealanders, most travelling around Africa picking up jobs with one of a plethora of extreme sports operators, or working for NGOs. She recalled having heard one of them say, 'Africa is the new Europe. Twenty years ago students would agree to meet up in Paris or Athens, now it's Vic Falls or Cape Town,' she didn't know if this was true, but she had seen the creep of Western influences: Nike trainers, McDonalds, car-chase American movies, and of course Coca Cola. While she thought the country, her country, was profiting, she worried the customs on which her nation had been founded would slowly disintegrate.

In the top right-hand corner of the menu were listed the *House Specialities*: giraffe, ostrich, warthog, kudu and crocodile. Romance must have muttered 'crocodile' almost under her breath.

'You need to be wary of croc. It's cut from the tail. It can be subject to salmonella,' Kingsley cautioned delicately.

'No, I was just taking my time to read it all. To be honest, I don't think I've even seen half of these animals, and as for eating them, well …' she allowed her voice to trail off.

'Do you know what it tastes like, Kingsley?' Mr Simons asked.

'Chicken with a hint of fish, is what everyone says. But the farmed croc I think is a little more subtle. And the texture is different,' he explained.

When the waitress returned with their bottles of soft drink, Kingsley ordered grilled fish, Romance played safe with chicken, and Mr Simons decided to risk the flame-grilled croc.

'Will you ask the chef to make sure the crocodile is cooked right through?' Kingsley asked the waitress, as she was walking away. Then, turning to Mr Simons, 'We can't spare you again, Mr Simons: the business needs you. And with Christmas just around the corner, the crews will not applaud so loudly if their bonuses are late.'

'Please, I'd like it if you would both call me Stephen,' Mr Simons said, smiling at them both. 'And you'll be pleased to know I agreed the bonuses with Mr Robertson a month or more ago. I think everyone will be pleased. It's been a good year, as I'm sure you are aware from the mountain of work you handle.'

The restaurant filled slowly. Kingsley said hello to a couple of the black guys who were in parties with white work colleagues from offices close by, or had come into town from one of the outlying lodges. The black business community, looking to enjoy a formal lunch, tended to favour one of the hotel restaurants out along the river, where the food was served in air-conditioned coolness. Only the whites seemed to believe that a braai wafting smoke, casually dressed staff, and an audience of monkeys in the overhead trees plotting to snatch away their own lunch, was aspirational.

While they waited for their food, they discussed how the business was going and what problems they should expect to be facing in the New Year. Romance considered to herself that this was probably her first business lunch, and smiled.

Stephen decided that next time he would order the giraffe, in the hope that the portion might be bigger. And Romance agreed to chocolate fondant ice cream, before her diet nudged her to refuse.

'Kingsley, I'd like to thank you again for your quick action in telephoning Mr Robertson. I'm sure if the solicitor hadn't been so fast off the mark, I'd still be languishing in one of this country's prisons.'

'Justice in this country, Stephen, is really quite good. But like many other things, particularly in government, the wheels turn very slowly,' Kingsley explained, dropping the use of his boss's surname name in his stride.

'I still don't quite understand what it was all about. Who was the poor woman? And who were the two men I now understand did the killing, and have fled to Zaire or Angola, or wherever?'

Kingsley hesitated, looked at Romance tentatively before speaking, and then answered thoughtfully. 'Like most things in this country, not everything is transparent. Rumour has it that the dead woman was the sister of our client Mr Fumina, but I am of the opinion that she was in fact the sister of his ex-business partner. I think she must have known that Mr Fumina was going to be out of the country for most of the year, so when her husband died she asked if she could stay at the villa for a few weeks. I think she ended up living there for a year or more. Whether Mr Fumina knew she had remained, I do not know.'

'That sort of explains who she was, but who were her killers, and why did they kill her?' Stephen enquired, then added, 'A robbery gone wrong, I suppose.'

Romance did not know what Kingsley would answer: if he would lie, or what. She only now realized where the conversation was heading, and she was sure Kingsley would be aware that she would be ill at ease in a discussion on the subject. It was not something that she had previously considered, and was not the sort of gossip that she would have overheard in the shops. Probably this was a weekly, maybe a daily occurrence, nevertheless it still remained an unspoken deed. She looked around for a sign indicating the direction of the *Ladies*, without success.

'Please excuse me, Mr Stephen, Kingsley,' she said, not feeling sufficiently at ease to simply use her boss's first name, but retaining the 'Mr', in the African tradition.

Romance left Kingsley to say what he considered most appropriate. As she weaved her way between the tables her mind went back to the traditions she valued, and then to those rituals she believed were wrong. She looked at the customers she was passing: most were European. Some things were wrong, but were these the people she wanted to influence the changes.

'The talk is that she slipped away from her village immediately after her husband's funeral. The headman ordered her back. When she refused, he sent two of his henchmen out to find her and bring her back by force. When they eventually found her, and persuasion failed, it seems things got out of hand and she was killed.' Kingsley stated in a calm, matter-of-fact manner.

'But why would they kill her?' Stephen persisted, frowning at the incomprehension of the affair rattling around in his head.

'Drugs, maybe … People do bad things,' Kingsley replied, having taken the decision not to expand the thought. Most Europeans did not understand, and many Africans felt the way he did. Ashamed.

'A rumble in the jungle,' Stephen said, turning his head skyward in response to the brontide.

Kingsley understood the boxing reference. Almost instantly doughnut-shaped rain spots, mirroring the wine glass ring stains, splashed down onto the table, abruptly bringing the main thread of the conversation to an end. Stephen and Kingsley, along with the other customers who had finished their meals, darted into the building. A number of those still dining lifted the tables in teams and squeezed them into the tight space close to the bar where the thin thatch sticks were supplemented with sheets of clear Perspex, then continued eating. Stephen was not sure why they had taken cover at all. The office had to be reopened, and from the full clouds hanging overhead, it was clear they were in for a soaking.

Having exited the toilet, Romance was dwarfed by an army, mainly of men with bare, hairy, brown legs, neutral-coloured shirts and a variety of head gear, ranging from baseball caps embroidered with tour company names to squares of cloth tied tight and knotted at the back, to leather fedoras. They were five or six deep. She decided not to 'excuse me, excuse me' all the way to the door. Instead she moved mouse-like around the wall, bumping into Mr Stephen and Kingsley halfway round considering their options.

'If you both would like to stay here until the storm is over, I can return to the office. I have an umbrella,' Romance suggested, attempting to pull her collapsible umbrella from her bag, which was not proving as straightforward as it might under normal circumstances. Having elbowed the human barriers to the north, south and east of her, and received looks that varied from passing curiosity to irritation, she finally managed to pull the contraption free and made ready to inch her way in the direction of the door.

'Please, Romance,' Kingsley insisted, taking the umbrella from her. 'I will bring a truck over.'

Romance could not see him as he left. Buried deep in the human forest, she smiled at the sight he would be offering to the town, rushing back to the office with bent wires stretching the small piece of blue material over his head.

'Does it rain like this in England?' she asked, as much to break their silence as to know the answer.

Stephen had been looking at Romance and responded spontaneously, answering with a line from a Paul Simon song and thinking of a roly-poly girl.

'I do not understand, Mr Stephen.' A quizzical look spreading over her face.

'I'm sorry, Romance, I was miles away. It rains a lot, particularly in my part of the country, but not normally like

41

this. Just long and slow.'

Romance noticed his face had coloured with embarrassment, but she did not understand why.

'Romance, tell me …' Stephen leaned a long way forward so that the people surrounding them could not overhear. 'The woman they thought I'd killed. Why would she be ordered back to her village by the headman? What was so wrong that she had to go into hiding? Had she had an affair? Or, did he think she was responsible for her husband's death?' He fired off the questions one after another, in conspiratorial whispers, worried about the reaction from his fellow diners if they knew of his arrest. 'No smoke without fire' would be their immediate thought, he understood that.

'What did Kingsley tell you?'

'He didn't, the storm broke before he had time to explain.'

Romance had been going to say that the country had many strange rituals, but changed her mind. 'Mr Stephen, some things in this country are difficult for foreigners to understand. We have many traditions that have been passed down many generations.'

'I'm sure hacking young ladies to death is not one of them, Romance.'

Stephen had left the way open for Romance to elaborate, but it was not an opportunity she chose to develop.

Kingsley returned, flustered and wet, with his shirt sticking to his skin. Brandishing a number of company logo'd golfing umbrellas, he shepherded his colleagues to the waiting truck, before going back and offering the same service to a number of other diners who had cars parked close by, which was very much a Kingsley gesture.

Over the following few days Stephen opened conversations with both Kingsley and Romance that did not involve company business and on each occasion, when his interest moved in the direction of the killing, he felt their chats cool, and reasons were found to avoid the topic. He could not fathom whether their resistance to openly discuss the subject was due to the character of the dead woman or the identity of her slayers, or to do with him personally, although this last option seemed unlikely as in all other matters his relationship with them both seemed without malice. Eventually, he decided to give up his digging and broach the matter with Sanjay Johal when their paths crossed again in the future.

oOo

Rarely did Romance pull the bottom drawer of her wardrobe completely out. Having secured the front door, she ensured the curtains were tightly closed, which was difficult as the amount of skinny yellow flowered material barely stretched the width. She coaxed the drawer off the runners with jagged movements, the timber swollen in the damp atmosphere, and allowed it gently to come to rest on the floor in front of her. Using a small torch to light the patch of floor now exposed, she scratched away at the area of previously disturbed earth and removed a small canister from the neatly dug hole Kunda had made when she had first moved in.

It took all her energy to unscrew the lid, as it had taken all her energy to tighten it on her last visit. From it she removed a large wad of American dollars, in an assortment of denominations. As she counted quietly in her head, a great feeling of warmth and security grew within her. From her bag she took the envelope containing the entirety of her December wages and removed well over half the notes, holding back the smallest amount she believed she would need to see her through the coming month, to buy some small Christmas gifts for those she wanted to thank for their kindness over the past twelve months, and to purchase something special for Kunda. Then, of course, there was the cost of the bus ticket for her long journey back to the village. At the last moment she retrieved one extra note, deciding to find herself something nice to wear so her husband would be proud of her when they went out. With her usual diligence, she replaced the canister and swept away any sign of unusual activity in the surrounding area.

The following morning she woke early, but rose late. It was Saturday and she had booked the whole day off to make all her arrangements. It had not been her intention to sleep in, but the sound of sheets of rain lashing down outside offered her the opportunity of a small luxury she seldom afforded herself. Her one worry was that all the nice dresses the woman on the stall had told her would be arriving today, would be sold. But she comforted herself with the thought that many other shoppers would not have ventured out to buy nice things in such inclement weather.

Angry with herself, it was a little after three by the time she stood in the travel office at the bus station, buying her ticket for the bus leaving at six a.m. on Christmas Eve. A seat on the bus was more important than a dress, she had decided, and it was probably the right decision as the clerk had told her there were now only a few seats remaining. The break in the downpour that had shown its face an hour earlier did not last, and before she had reached the market the water was falling from the sky, turning the gutters into boiling pots every bit as turbulent as she felt. Being caught in the rain today was not such a disaster, as had been the case for more rainy seasons than she could remember – each year begrudging the purchase of a new umbrella. The badly disfigured excuse she had loaned Kingsley had lasted well, but she smiled proudly as she hoisted the company logo above her head and recalled the pleasure on Mr Stephen's face when he had presented her with it as a gift. 'Can't have you parading around with that inadequate piece of antiquity,' he had told her. 'Besides, you'll be a good

44

advertisement for the company.'

The hundred or more market stalls were protected by walls of tarpaulin rolled from their tops, but aloft they were bowed, ready to split with the gallons of water they had collected. As an additional safeguard, the stallholders had covered their wares with sheets of once clear, but now opaque, polythene, which made it almost impossible to evaluate the goods on offer. Romance was a regular shopper in the market and quickly moved through the rows of food, into the hardware area and then beyond to the thirty or more traders offering rails of clothing, linen and bales of material for making dresses, curtains and a whole imagination of soft furnishings. Needlework, Romance would be the first to admit, was not one of the skills she had succeeded in mastering. But maybe, she thought, when they had their new house and she was pregnant, she would try really hard.

Flanked by a number of stalls selling fake designer garments, the largest offering was of secondhand clothes imported from Europe. Romance lowered her umbrella and stepped expectantly in, under the awning. It took her barely a few moments to realize that there was only a little more stock than she had seen set out the previous week. Disappointed, she wondered whether she should go to the store and look there, but she knew that the items would be of poorer quality and she would have to increase her budget. Without enthusiasm, she decided to stay and look.

'Sha, hallo.' Romance glanced round to see who was addressing her. 'Are you winning?' the small woman asked, lifting herself slowly from the low stool positioned behind the back trestle.

'Losing,' Romance replied, catching sight of the woman. 'I'm still trying to find a dress for seeing my husband at Christmas, but you have nothing,' she added miserably, with a hint of accusation in her tone: a promise previously made but now not fulfilled.

'Sha, I didn't forget you. I thought of my friend the moment I saw it, and I keep it for you.'

Bending down, she pulled a blue mini-market plastic bag from under the trestle and brought it round to Romance.

'Look, your husband will not be able to take his eyes off you,' she said, pulling out a neatly folded lemon-yellow dress.

Romance knew her eyes had lit up the moment she had seen it unfurl, spying the Givenchy label only a split second later. 'How much?' she asked enviously, considering her budget before daring to reach out and take it from the stallholder's outstretched arm.

'Sha, you take it home and try it on. If it fits and you want it, we can arrange a price.' The stallholder saw Romance's worried face. 'If you pay hard, not local, it will not be too much.' The woman took the dress back, folded it carefully, replaced it in the bag and handed it to her customer. 'It will be perfect, you see.'

Romance liked the woman and wondered if it was because she was one of few people small enough to look up to her, and reminded her of a female version of the church organist. She took the bag and held it close, to ensure it benefited from full protection against the rain.

o0o

Standing in front of her mirror, Romance slipped into the dress for the second time. Nervous to have taken on more expense than she had intended, she looked herself up and down and twirled around. She decided it looked even better than it had when she had first tried it on and had made the decision to spend whatever the stallholder demanded. Greenbacks had exchanged hands, both parties pleased with the outcome.

'Sha, you did not need to return today,' the stallholder had told her.

But having taken the decision, Romance felt she had to pay before there was any chance she would truly consider the cost.

On the third appraisal, Romance's line of vision caught sight of a small folded sheet of paper that had been pushed under her door. She was surprised she had not seen it before, but in all her excitement she knew it might well have been lying there even when she returned to try the dress on for the first time.

Picking up the letter, she now felt guilty that the American dollars she had used to purchase the dress could have been sent to her sister to buy much-needed drugs. Maybe it was too late for medicine. Why had Sonkwe not stopped? Was he too ashamed? Maybe it was not Sonkwe who had delivered it. Retreating to the bed, Romance sat back heavily, and then immediately jumped to her feet. Again, she felt guilty that the care of her dress had taken precedence over the news she held in her hand.

Carefully she pulled the dress over her head and hung it on her clothes rail, covering it with a sheet of plastic the stallholder had given her. In her bra and pants, she climbed onto the bed and began to read, tears rolling down her cheeks as her eyes traced the poorly scrawled words along the three lines of writing.

Sunday, she stayed at home, missing church for the second time in a month. She lay in bed, and even the sight of her new dress did nothing to lift her spirits. In fact, the very existence of it brought sadness to her heart. She buried her sobs in a pillow which, by lunchtime, was so wet it might have been used to patch a hole in the roof.

By Monday, when she came to sit at her desk in the office, Romance had pulled herself together after scolding herself for being so sentimental.

'I have to go out at lunchtime,' Romance announced to Kingsley and Mr Stephen, who she had managed to speak to when they were standing together by Kingsley's desk. 'If I go at twelve, will that be alright?' she asked.

'Perfect,' Stephen replied. 'Are you going to get something nice?' he asked.

'No, I want to see if I can get a refund on my ticket. I got a note on Saturday from Kunda telling me he had to work over Christmas and that I should not come.' she told them with a touch of near menace in her voice, then added with a tinge of hope, 'He said he would visit me here in the New Year.'

When she returned from her ticket errand her anger had spread. The man in the ticket office had refused to give her money back. Another person in the queue offered to purchase it from her, and was abruptly told by the clerk that tickets were not transferable. Romance had banged the desk, and the prospective purchaser had shouted at the ridiculousness of such a rule, demanding to see a book of terms and conditions where it was stated. People further back in the line then became agitated for fear of missing their bus, and the whole episode turned into a near-riot. Finally, Romance had been offered a credit note, which with some reluctance she had accepted.

'I had been going to ask Kingsley to pop in from time to time over the holiday,' Stephen told her, 'and I was going to keep an eye out during the night,' he added, 'But if you're going to be staying in town, maybe it's something you could do. It would allow me to attend to a couple of drinks invitations I would have otherwise missed, and it would boost your pay cheque.'

Romance considered the opportunity and frowned.

'I do not think I would like to walk unaccompanied in the early hours of the morning to the office and back,' she said with consideration.

While there was no real history of attacks or muggings taking place in the centre of the town – in fact it was generally considered one of the safer areas – walking between hotels and lodges alone on the outskirts of town, or close to the river bank, was not recommended. But this mainly applied to tourists, and few were so stupid; if anything, most were over-cautious. Ridiculously so, in her opinion.

'There is the flat upstairs that Mr Robertson uses. You could stay there. That would be the best solution all round,' Stephen told her, clearly pleased with the idea.

Romance liked the thought of staying upstairs. It was nice accommodation. After Mr Robertson had left, the opportunity had been taken to redecorate the place, and she had let the painters in and locked up after they had left. It had a large bath in the bathroom, a proper kitchen, and colour television. Without Kunda, on her own in her dark little room, she was visualizing a miserable time. She agreed.

Later, in the afternoon, a worry began to loom up and she was now not sure she had made the right decision. There was little work outstanding, so she spent the time worrying. Then she thought of a solution to her problem.

Kingsley smiled, always pleased to be of assistance.

'Of course you can, Romance. Stephen has a key, which he keeps at home in a safe there, and Mr Robertson has a key in England, but I'm the only person here with a key and I'm the only one who uses the safe.'

The following day, with the office closed for the Christmas holiday, Kingsley collected Romance from her room along with her small case she had packed for her trip north – but without the Givenchy dress, which remained sadly under plastic. Deep in her shoulder-bag she had buried the large, folded brown envelope she had taken from work and used to pack her savings, which she had been fearful of leaving in their hiding place during her extended absence.

Before carrying her case upstairs, she watched as Kingsley pushed her package out of harm's way to the back of the safe, turned the key in the door, and tugged at it to

49

show Romance that it was securely locked. He hugged her, which was not the sort of thing he normally did, wished her a happy Christmas, and promised to look in to make sure everything was well with her.

Upstairs, she was surprised to find Mr Stephen sitting at the kitchen table.

CHAPTER FOUR

'Hey, Bulongo. Get me a Shake Shake.' The man sitting at
the long trestle table called loudly above the throbbing
noise that vibrated the beer hall, beaming a grin at his friend
who was heading for a long wait at the three-deep line along
the bar. All men, orderly, taking turns, but lively as they
were calling out to others waiting who they knew,
exchanging greetings or good-humoured insults. There was
a lot of waving of notes to attract service to one section
being ignored in favour of another.

It took ten minutes before he arrived and placed two
cartons of Shake Shake on the table in front of his friend.
Isaac shuffled along the seat, making room on the bench
next to him.

'Sit, sit,' Isaac gestured, as the good-looking young man,
whose lean frame was showing signs of a good life, placed
his own two bottles of Mosi beer on the table. The trestle
construction was already a shambles of empties and
overflowing tins that served as ashtrays.

'Two each, Bulongo – it's good to have rich friends,'
Isaac said, shaking the first of the cartons before pouring
out the opaque liquid. Many simply tore the top and drank,

but Isaac liked drinking the industrially produced traditional beer from a glass. By the time he had done this, his friend had already downed half of his first bottle almost in a single gulp. The gas, and the speed of his swallow, caused him to belch loudly the moment he took the neck away from his mouth. Isaac laughed.

'Why you sit at a black table?' Bulongo asked.

'You find a clean one, lucky to get a seat at all when it's this busy.'

Bulongo pushed his forearm along the table just above the surface, so as not to ruin his sleeve, moving glasses and bottles out of their way. Drinkers further down gave him a stare, but then went back to their own worlds.

Three hundred people, mainly young men, packed the hall. The smell of alcohol, tobacco and dagga smoke, and revellers' sweat, attacked the nostrils as violently as the noise did the ears. As consumption continued and the night wore on, vision would become a similar casualty. But it was still early, and pockets pouted with Christmas bonuses.

A six-piece band on the stage, touring on the road from Jo'burg, were powering out their material – some original songs, other popular South African classics, punctuated by the occasional Mali number in French. The music was appreciated, but as the hours grew it was the drinking and joking of the audience that moved to centre stage. By one o'clock, as many sat stretched out on the dusty concrete floor as lounged in chairs, or were squeezed on benches. Trips to the bar often ended in arguments as seats were immediately snatched when vacated.

Isaac left, more than a little drunk, long before his friend, who would not be persuaded, insisting the Christmas holiday had begun, and he did not have work for the next eight days. He stumbled between various groups, some he had known most of his life. They pushed bottles of spirit into his hand to chug-a-lug from the neck, or passed freshly rolled or already well-smoked dagga for him to suck the smoke deep into his lungs. But much of the energy had left shortly after Isaac. It was the time of night that seemed to be a tipping point the world over with physical capability quicker than mental ambition. He stumbled against a girl close to the stage who he had noticed when he had first arrived, and she was still alone. He roughly fondled her right breast during the collision, and breathed the offer of a drink. Pushing him away, she spat in his face and laughed as a bottle kicked by her man on stage smacked him in the side of the head. Reeling, he jostled his way in the direction of the doors, camouflaged in the crowd for fear of further missiles.

'You want to fuck me, Bulongo?' a woman three times his weight asked, as he crashed onto the end of a bench next to her. 'You have money?' she enquired, turning her attention from the man next to her who looked as though he had passed out hours before, and now lay with his large pock-marked cheek marinating in an emulsion of Shake Shake, ash and saliva on the trestle top. As she eased herself closer to him, her new object of desire, he felt the bench react to the shift in weight. Grabbing savagely at the dough of her upper arm he pulled himself erect and tumbled away.

'You know where to find me, Bulongo?' she called to the sweat-drenched shirt retreating in front of her.

Outside, the rain, which had earlier almost drowned out the band with violent patters pounding the tin roof, had stopped. The hard dirt was now soft and mud, tinged red from the traces of copper in the earth, squelched under the soles of his new shoes.

There were now almost as many people outside as he had left behind. People mingled, hugged, continued to down beverages, take smoke into their lungs, piss in corners, start their unsteady walk into the township or out along the main highway. Cars sent up soft spray as they vied to escape the car park through both the In and Out designated openings.

Confused. Where he imagined he had parked his car, it was nowhere to be seen. He parked in the same space regularly when buying from the supermarket that adjoined the beer hall. The neon sign, the only one locally, which was as much a display of the owner's wealth as it was a pointer into the lot, was dark. But even without that light, he was not crazy. A Hiace van glupped mud up his leg as it passed. He sat on the wall pondering the theft of his pride and joy, and rolled a joint. This, he was sure, would calm his nerves and aid his memory.

o0o

'Get that heap of shit out of here before I have it towed and give you the bill.'

Thin lapels, broad shoulders, and the chin. He did not need to see the full face of the man hammering on the roof of his car. Sun streamed in, burning his eyes. He was stretched uncomfortably across the back seat. It was quiet for a moment, then a single heavy slap on the metal shook the car and blistered his eardrum. He winced. A face, zipped with perfect white teeth, peered in.

'Bulongo, you look as though you had a win last night. I'm going to park my car. Make sure you're out of here by the time I get back.'

Pulling himself into a sitting position, he watched Jacob purr the large, shiny late-model black Mercedes across the car park to the concreted loading area, and the parking bay reserved for the boss. Jacob was not someone you wanted to get on the wrong side of. He hadn't become the owner of the two best money-making machines in the township purely with business acumen. Opening the door, it all came flooding into his head.

'Fuck ... Fuck.'

He dropped heavily into the front seat, and adjusted the rear-view mirror to scan his face. His black skin looked grey, his eyes were bloodshot through. He poked his tongue at himself and scratched the surface coating with a fingernail, then gagged on whatever it was that was on his finger.

'Fuck,' he repeated.

He couldn't even remember if he had used a condom. He couldn't remember very much at all. She was hardly kaleza: thin as a razor blade she was not. The thought went through his head that she might even be the antidote to AIDS. He smiled at his witticism. He looked down at the front of his trousers and saw the zip was broken. His clothes were red with large splodges of mud; he thought he must have fallen. The cream cloth on the back seat had been the real victim, and then he recalled her snatching more money from him when she saw the red stains and smears over her yellow dress.

'Her, anyone but her,' he mumbled as the engine turned over and he headed out onto the road, away from the township, in the direction of the village.

He had been hoping to find a girl he had seen a few weeks back dancing to kwaito music, all energy, slender, not with the big boulders that had nearly suffocated him while he was pinned down on the back seat. The dancing girl was not someone he had seen around previously, but he was sure she was a chicken. He would have happily paid double for her.

The brakes screeched as he stamped his wet shoe to the floor, threw the door open, was blasted by a following truck he had not seen, and jack-knifed almost in half as he emptied his stomach by the side of the road. The stretch of road was as busy as usual; long-distance truck drivers sped fast past him to be at their destination and share at least some of the festive holiday with their families. He rested on the bonnet, oblivious to the constant sound of horns as vehicles swerved to avoid him. A bakkie flashed its lights and pulled up behind him. Isaac was the last person he wanted to see.

'Are you winning?' Isaac grinned as he walked around the outside of the car, stepping over the pool of vomit as he went.

His question went unanswered. Isaac opened the passenger door, pulled back quickly, and closed off the offending smell with a slam.

'Shit that clunks. I think the chicken you fucked in there must have been dead,' Isaac said, pulling a face.

Then he slapped his friend on the shoulder and laughed.

'Who was she, Bulongo?'

'A new girl,' he lied, choking his fear rather than his hope.

'I was going to offer to drive you home. But clunking like that my sha ...' Isaac did not finish the sentence.

He slapped him on the back again and returned to the bakkie.

The guy behind the wheel drove Isaac with respect, but by the time Bulongo got himself together, opened all the windows and pulled back out into the traffic, the bakkie was long gone. Weaving out around lorries crammed full of people, cars and taxis, he wrenched the steering wheel hard to the left to avoid head-on collisions. He was determined to pass Isaac before they both pulled off the tarmac, onto the mud and cinder track that led to Zimwani Lodge, and their village.

'Bastard!' he yelled out at a driver who made no effort to accommodate the closing space he found himself negotiating as an oncoming truck, lights flashing, pounded its horn.

He reached the turn-off at almost the same moment as Isaac, threw the wheel left and immediately right, bouncing, without consideration for the suspension, in much the same way he remembered his experience of the previous night, in and out of potholes, and grinning at his friend as he passed, peppering the air with a fog of sludge and grit.

A mile further on he pulled off on a side track, which headed away from the lodge and towards the village. Slowing, not wanting to attract attention, or having to explain his current state. He parked up not far from the toilet block, and waved a British five-pound note in the face of the lad charged with the task of keeping the toilets and showers clean – an impossible job, unless undertaken with a lot more ambition than the lad possessed. Quickly returning the inducement to his pocket, he expressed his wish to see his car returned to its immaculate state.

Inside the darkness of his traditional thatched hut, he stripped and, using a torch, inspected the minutiae of his penis at some length. Satisfied there was no sign of impairment or sickness, he fell onto his bed, rolled himself a joint, downed a Mosi, and slept through that day and the greater part of Christmas Day.

CHAPTER FIVE

Kitchen pans clashed. Romance held one in each hand and smashed them together hard and fast. It was the only thing she could think of doing. The din exploded, sending shock-waves around the lit room and out into the darkened yard below. In the night all other sounds were subdued, but in response to her alarm, dogs began to bark and windows nearby became white with light. Below in the yard, the muted attack on the assets of the business burst from its secrecy as the thieves flew into confusion.

Romance had been sleeping lightly, half awake, half dreaming of nice things, when she felt herself stiffen in the bed. At first she thought the noise was imagined, part of her dream. But then she was sure: she recognized the sound of the chain falling away, albeit a little muffled, and the scraping of the corrugated tin on the gate as it passed over the uneven broken tarmac. In the dark, leaving her bed, she eased open the window to confirm her fears. Soft footfalls, and the movement of shadows darting around between the trucks. She was sure a figure was at the door of the chemical shed. Frozen, she shouted at the intruders, but no words, no voice left her throat. Then she worried that if the men below realized they had been seen, they might try to grab and silence her. How, she was not sure, but it was in her mind now. Easing herself away, she crept into the kitchen and lifted the phone – then remembered it was an extension that had to be connected to the outside world from the switchboard downstairs on her desk. She appreciated that if she did not hurry everything would be stolen, and the thieves would be long gone before anything could be done to stop them. It was at that point she turned on the light and grabbed the saucepans.

Kingsley was the first to arrive. Romance was continuing to applaud her own success, although with less vigour.

'You can stop now, Romance,' Kingsley told her, placing his arm around her shoulder. 'Whoever they were, they've gone now. From the quick look I had on the way in, nothing's been taken.'

'I've dented both pans,' Romance admitted as she laid them both on the kitchen table. 'I'll see if the man in the market can tap the dents out, or maybe I must just buy new.'

'I don't think either will be necessary,' Mr Simons assured her, making her jump as he approached without her recognizing his footfall. 'You've done wonderfully: if you hadn't been here and taken the action you did, the yard would have been cleared out.'

'But the pans ...' Romance said, looking at their shapes, which seemed now to resemble British fifty-pence pieces.

'I'm sure the company can withstand the loss of a couple of pans. Now, would you like me to make you a cup of tea – or I do have a bottle of whisky in the office drawer downstairs?'

Mr Simons decided for her. 'Three whiskies, I think.'

'No, no, Kingsley is a Muslim. He doesn't drink alcohol anymore,' Romance blurted out in a panic.

'I'll bring him a soft drink from the fridge. Two whiskies and a soft it is, then,' Mr Simons said, smiling to himself.

Romance fell into a wooden kitchen chair and dropped her head into her hands, exhausted.

'Where is Kingsley?' Romance asked, suddenly worried by his absence when Mr Simons returned, glasses and bottles and a packet of shortbread biscuits precariously balanced on a tray.

'Just finishing securing the yard.'

Later, Mr Simons, having replenished their drinks, a statement and a 'Christmas box' offered and accepted by the uniformed policeman who had been called out to record the incident, Romance found herself sitting, slightly drunk but alone, on her bed: watching the television and wishing her husband had not been required to work. The opportunity for him to boost their savings with the substantial amount of tips was small solace.

The next day Romance cleaned the small flat in every corner, and along every ledge, providing extra elbow grease in the areas Mr Robertson's cleaner had skirted over on many past visits. Then she went down to her office area and gave it similar attention. Next, using the luxury of the washing machine, she washed all her dirty clothes and those she calculated would be dirty before long. They dried quickly between downpours of rain, on a makeshift line she erected in the yard. She took the opportunity to check the gates Kingsley had securely fastened still remained so. In the evening, having ironed all her clothing, she ran a deep bath and began the process all over again, but this time focusing on herself.

The following morning, late, the last day before everyone was back at work and the town's commercial activities returned to normal, Mr Simons called into the office and asked Romance if she would join him for lunch, if she had nothing else planned. On this occasion, eating in the same restaurant where she had eaten with him previously, Romance was more confident and, accepting a glass of wine, she felt almost relaxed.

'I've spoken to Mr Robertson and he thinks it would be a good idea, if you had no objection, for you to move into the flat on a permanent basis, or at least for the foreseeable future,' he waited for her to reply and to gauge her response.

'I'm not sure,' she said, using her fork to push the remaining pieces of food around her plate. 'Where will I stay when Mr Robertson visits?' Romance asked, less interested in the answer, more concerned at the cost of the flat and the extra expense of the power for the labour-saving devices she knew she would not be able to resist. And then there was Kunda: would she be allowed to have him stay when he visited? 'No it is not practical,' she said, stabbing a now soggy chip, with no intent of lifting it to her mouth, let alone eating it.

'Romance, if you think about it, it's extremely practical. You won't have to pay rent and the company will pay your living expenses, and in return we'll get the security of having someone on site 24/7. Crime isn't getting any less.' Romance looked at the gouge marks on his wrists and thought of the woman who had stood next to her in church for over a year. 'Mr Robertson is convinced, and I have to say I agree with him,' Mr Simons added.

'And what happens when my husband comes? Will he be allowed to stay?'

'Of course, Romance. It will be your home. And consider it an endorsement of the company's satisfaction with your performance.'

Romance knew she wanted to take advantage of the offer, but something was stopping her grabbing the opportunity with both hands. She didn't know what, a feeling, something nagged. Then, on the other hand, there were Sonkwe's words about the squalor of her accommodation, when he delivered the last letter from her sister: this stabbed at her.

'I will stay and see how I get on, but I am not going to give up my room until I'm sure,' she said in a decisive manner, and added 'Thank you' in a softer tone.

After work the next day, Kingsley, who had offered to lend a hand and the use of his pickup, assisted Romance in moving most of her belongings from her room into the flat. A large tarpaulin from the yard, repelling rain that darkened the sky long before the dusk was due … pink and white laundry bags … black garbage bags, and boxes not wet from the yard … Kingsley carried and deposited each in the appropriate room designated by Romance.

'It is strange how little you think you have until you come to move. Is it like that for everyone, do you think?' Romance contemplated as Kingsley's journeys up and down stairs reached double figures.

'Everything has a value, so people find it difficult to throw things out. But usually many of the items have a greater value for people who do not possess them. My wife and I do not have great needs, so we try to give things we do not use greatly to people who will get greater use or pleasure from them,' Kingsley explained.

'You are a good man Kingsley, and thank you for helping me.'

'It was nothing, but in truth your husband should be by your side assisting you,' Kingsley said, with only a slight hint of disapproval.

'The shop owner was very annoyed when I went back to collect the last few things. I think he thought you were leaving without giving notice. I assured him you would continue to pay the rent. I hope that was the truth,' he told her after setting down the final box.

'Even though I am sure it's far too high, and he would have difficulty finding someone else to rent it at the price I pay. And he has a month's deposit. But yes, that was right; I am keeping it at least for a while. And when I am ready to leave I will let him know,' Romance said, already begrudging paying for a room for which she had no use.

CHAPTER SIX

He had insisted that she drop the 'Mr'. Just 'Stephen' was fine. Sitting in the passenger seat next to him after service on Sunday, she accepted it was not work. But, in her head, it felt another step outside what she had envisaged when she had started her working life: calling her boss by his first name. It was about respect, not simply for the person but also for the position.

The eye of the preacher was not lost on her, as he watched from the church steps when she climbed into the cab next to a smartly dressed young, white man. He would also not have missed Stephen's welcoming smile as he greeted her: a smile she returned without a second thought. She hoped the man of God would not interpret this as a sign of her availability, and renew his lurid suggestions the next time he shook hands with thanks for her attendance.

Romance always liked the feel of the town on a Sunday, particularly on dry days. She sat quietly looking out. Many men wore suits, substituting jeans or overalls, the women in flowery dresses and children, proud in their blazered school uniforms, replacing the more casual ensembles advocated by some schools for weekday attendance. Many were completing their duty of prayer and, like Romance and Stephen, were now cheerfully spending the remainder of the day with friends, or eating fast food and ice cream, which the young children demanded excitedly. Romance, self-consciously, had worn her new dress to church, the one she had bought for Kunda, and Christmas. It had been Kingsley's solution to her feeble excuse for not going, when she claimed she did not have anything suitable to wear. Even with a coat on, she had seen the preacher's eyes settle on the smallest promise of exposed cleavage.

As the scattering of larger buildings, housing, shops, schools and commercial enterprises, dwindled, a few modern low-level constructions began to sprout, set back off the road with manicured landscapes and designed signage. Stephen called it 'Tescoville' and smiled, but she could not fathom his amusement. Within a few hundred yards, this prosperity petered out in favour of family dwellings: part-completed buildings on small plots that would progress as money became available to purchase the sand and cement needed to mould the breeze blocks.

Seven weeks into the New Year, the rains had eased; some predicted there would be no more, for a while at least. Three days had passed without a storm, but nothing was certain. Certainly, the handkerchief squares of cultivated land and the vast tracts of bush were deep green; vegetable crops above the ground were bulbous. Romance immediately thought of her pots in the yard outside her old room, that she had not been back to harvest. How quickly one accepts change, she reflected.

On the left, a small hand-painted sign was coming into view. Cut in the shape of an outboard motor tipped on its side, it pointed off the main road along a track which could easily otherwise have been missed. Stephen slowed and turned. Romance began to bounce in her seat, at one time grabbing Stephen's arm to save herself. She released her grip quickly without speaking, and Stephen slowed to a crawl.

'Welcome to my home.' Kingsley, dressed in a light grey linen suit, greeted them and then quickly moved to receive two more guests, who had followed Stephen and Romance along the track in a new, highly polished Range Rover. Stephen knew no one amongst those congregated in various sized clumps, like groups of shrubs. He recognized a few, from brushing shoulders at the bank in town, but nobody to strike up in conversation. Romance knew many of the less affluent by sight, and some would have engaged her if she had approached. But shyness prevented her from taking a step closer to the party, and more importantly she foresaw the responsibility would have been on her shoulders to introduce Stephen: Mr Stephen, Stephen Simons, her boss. They would draw conclusions, incorrectly, conclusions she would not want to become speculation. Held still, Stephen and Romance struggled silently with their awkwardness. Stephen gently cleared his throat and opened his mouth to speak to her.

'I am sorry to have left you like that, more people seem to be arriving than RSVP'd the invitations,' Kingsley apologized, returning at that precise moment. Romance handed him a small wrapped parcel, a book by an African author, she had purchased in the market. She guessed it had probably been left by a guest at one of the lodges. The stallholder recommended it for its binding and good leather cover. Stephen gifted a small electronic organizer he had ordered in from South Africa.

'Excuse me a moment, I would just like to thank everyone and announce that the buffet is open.' Kingsley apologized again, taking a couple of steps away and tapping a piece of stick on a table to gain attention.

'Today is a very happy day for me. It's my thirtieth birthday, my fifth wedding anniversary and, yesterday, my father received an order for our one hundred and first canoe since opening the business three years ago,' Kingsley announced proudly as he addressed the small crowd. 'My wife and I, and my mother and father, would like to thank you all for joining us in our home to celebrate this occasion with us. There is food being served from the kitchen, so please make yourself at home.'

His guests gave him a genuine round of applause, followed by a couple of choruses of 'Happy Birthday' led by someone Romance could not see. It was the first time Stephen had seen any touch of charisma in the personality of his bookkeeper.

As in the churches, most gatherings were motley, and Kingsley's guests did not disappoint. People who could provide influence were never without invitation. Bankers, council officials, lawyers and members of the security services, at all levels, were courted for their future favour.

Stephen assumed some were actually his customers, people Mr Robertson would have known well. But to him they were simply names and addresses. He made a mental note to go through the files, and visit the old established customers instead of always aggressively chasing the potentials.

Kingsley lingered, smiled, chatted, clasped hands with some and shook hands with others as he approached, grasping the thumb in the traditional African manner with others.

'I think there must be eighty people here,' he said as he surveyed around him, returning his attention to Stephen and Romance. 'Would you care to see my house?'

Proudly he first showed Romance and Stephen the large, single-storey workshop attached to the house. One half was shelved with neatly labelled used spare parts for outboard motors, and a large hook in the ceiling supported an engine that appeared to be undergoing work. The other portion was curtained off with plastic strips, where the ribbed carcass of a canoe awaited its covering.

'My father has repaired engines for most of his life, but

we only started the fibreglass business three years ago. I'm hoping to mould pool loungers next year. My father does most of the work, so it will depend on finding someone to trust as his assistant. I only have time to look after the books and control the ordering,' he explained, shrugging his shoulders. 'And I think actually my father enjoys the solitude of his work.'

Stephen eyed the height of the river, and the closeness to the back of the house, as Kingsley ushered them out through the rear door, snapping the lock closed on the outer metal gate.

'It is easy for thieves in canoes to approach the house when the river is this high,' Kingsley said by way of explanation.

The thought crossed Stephen's mind: the origin of the thieves' transport, and the correlation between that and the strength of the business.

'Don't wander too close: the people next door had a dog taken last week,' Kingsley warned Romance, who was picking her way around, with thought for her shoes, on the uneven bank.

'Canoeists?' Stephen enquired

'Crocs. More dogs are lost to crocs than anything,' Kingsley answered.

Both Stephen's and Romance's heads dropped in reflex to scan the outer edge of their path.

'Does the house flood? The water seems very high,' Stephen asked as they walked onto the back deck of the house.

'This is as high as it has been for a number of years. And it continues to rise a little, which means the rains in Angola are still quite heavy. You see the white foam on the water?' Stephen nodded. 'When that stops coming down the river, we will start to see the level dropping,' Kingsley explained.

At this time of the day, the deck roofing provided little shade. Most guests had remained at the front of the house, except for a young couple talking closely together in the knowledge their spoken feelings could not be overheard. They ignored their host as he passed, not out of rudeness but tunnel vision. Kingsley smiled at Stephen and Romance, and in low tones whispered: 'Romeo and Juliet.'

'Mr Simons,' Stephen recognized the voice, but momentarily could not place it. He turned to see who was addressing him and immediately smiled, taking the hand that was being extended in his direction. 'You're looking much better than when we last met. Are you keeping well, Stephen?'

'Mr Johal. Yes, extremely, thank you very much.'

'Sanjay, please. And no more infringements on your liberty, I assume,' his voice was softer than Stephen remembered, and his words understated. Obviously, a different demeanour than during his legal performances.

Kingsley guided Romance deeper into the house, in the direction of the kitchen. 'I had expected your husband to be with you, Romance.' Kingsley spoke in hushed tones, a troubled note in his voice. 'You know you were both invited.'

'I went to meet Kunda at the terminal. A passenger on the bus from my village relayed a message that Kunda was required to work. But he said he will come in three weeks.'

'I am sorry Romance. You do not seem to see very much of each other. I could not be separated from my wife for so long.'

'It doesn't make me happy,' she said, with no joy in her voice or her face.

Outside, Romance sat with Kingsley's mother and father. Complete opposites, both typically African, both typical stereotypes in their way. One big, one small. He was small, quiet and unassuming, with little to say. His wife – huge, smiling, with conversation that couldn't fail to turn a laugh. Romance at once decided that Kingsley took after his father, but on reflection wondered if, under his veneer, potentially more of his mother lurked than was daily expressed.

'Mr Simons.'

Stephen did not really understand why Kingsley had now addressed him formally.

'I would like to introduce you to my wife. Chipo, this is my boss, Mr Simons.'

Stephen had finished exchanging pleasantries with the lawyer and was standing in the kitchen with another ten or so people, eating or waiting to have their plates filled. The buffet appeared to offer an intriguing selection of colourful hot and cold dishes, filling the room with both pungent, and the hint of more subtle, aromas.

He had not noticed the young woman when he had first entered. Chipo was small and delicate, without seeming fragile. Her smile beamed from a perfect unblemished complexion, and her body was trim more than slim. She welcomed him into her home with words spoken sincerely and with perfect diction. Stephen felt he could not take his eyes off her and when their eyes met, hers danced playfully. With what seemed to require a determined effort, Stephen had returned his attention to his host for fear that his stare would be noticed and interpreted badly. It was not sexual interest: Chipo held a fascination he could not really explain. Watching her from a distance, in a conscious effort to identify the composition of what seemed to enthral him, he quickly became aware that she had the same effect on everyone she came close to. Kingsley was a very lucky man, Stephen decided, and wondered where he had found such a gem. Then he felt he understood why his employee seemed so content within himself.

Later, music played and a few people danced. Many of the more well-heeled invitees drifted, leaving the remainder of the party mostly to Kingsley's extended family, which appeared large, his neighbours and younger guests.

'It looks as though you're going to be in for a late night,'

Stephen noted as he thanked both Kingsley and Chipo for inviting him. 'If you'd like to take tomorrow off, you're very welcome.' Kingsley, ever conscientious, assured him that he would be at his desk as usual.

Romance had clearly enjoyed the party, chatting constantly on the drive back. Stephen wondered if the fruit cup on offer had been slightly stronger than Romance had realized.

True to his word, Kingsley was unlocking the front door before either Stephen had arrived or Romance had come down.

Overnight, the white foam on the river had all but vanished, and there were wet margins of grass along the high-water mark, giving rise to speculation among the yard workers that the level had started to drop. As if this were some clarion call, the telephone ringing kept Romance taking orders, booking equipment overhauls, and juggling work schedules for the service crews. Lodges on the islands and close to the river were eagerly programming in work for the arrival of green-season clients.

A week later, the foam was back and a deluge of water powering down from Angola advanced the river to within three feet of the decking at Kingsley's home.

CHAPTER SEVEN

The man felt himself subside. He waited a few moments, hot and wet with sweat, and then rolled away from the woman beneath him, sucking air deep into his lungs. She lay quietly, neither of them speaking, but he knew she wanted to roll on her side and be held close. She was looking for contact as well as sex.

'Your husband will be staying down in the Lower Zambezi for at least three weeks more. The water has risen again, so he won't be able to start work yet,' he said, remaining stretched out beside her. 'I have another week off and there's a truck going to Lusaka. We could party. I have friends we could stay with. There are some good clubs they go to and don't cost to get in.'

'Everyone would know, Bulongo.'

'You could get a bus and meet me there.'

'It would be nice to visit a city,' she said, turning into him and tasting the salt as she kissed his chest.

'You could drive me,' she suggested.

He had thought of taking the car, but there was the cost of petrol, the queues at gas stations that could last for hours, hanging around for the next tanker to deliver whatever little amount the forecourt owner could afford to pay upfront. And a serious chance, when he left the car anywhere after he'd been drinking, it would be stripped. If lucky, he would be offered the chance to buy the parts back. Then there was the constant shorty word up. When he drove, he liked to listen to music, not the incessant chattering women seemed to think is needed to fill the space.

'I have to go,' he said, starting to fidget.

'Not yet. Please,' she begged, and for persuasion, she straddled him, lowering her breasts onto his face. Instantly, she could feel he would stay.

oOo

'Hey Bulongo, someone tells me you have a nice little house in the village.' It was Isaac, coming out of the supermarket. 'And her husband is going to be away for many weeks.'

'You make me flat you talk like that man.' Bulongo's voice was angry. He looked around to see if anyone he knew was within earshot.

Isaac took a can from his carrier and pushed it into his friend's hand 'Here, strap down to the bus with me.'

Bulongo took the can, pulled the ring on it and took a deep swallow, but refused the walk to the bus stop, heading instead for the beer hall. His little house was becoming more like some big house. She was meant to be at his beck and call, not the other way round. The sooner her husband returned the better, he decided. Before he left her, she had changed her mind again and agreed she would go with him to the city.

The village was small: twenty huts scattered without a plan in an area of cleared bush. He wondered if he should move into the township, find a room. It would be easier not to have everyone watching his every move, live on a street with a few hundred people. It was a thought.

Finding that the door refused to budge after a number of determined shakes, he looked at his watch and realized it was only eleven-thirty. The sun was hot today, and as he finished the can he wished he had pushed Isaac for a second.

'You're in a hurry to get started, sha.' The new chicken he had seen working in the beer hall at Christmas had appeared from around the other side of the building. 'I have beer at my place, cold, if you want to spend your money.'

He imagined her naked, which was not difficult. The dress she wore was peachy-coloured, and the material clung statically to her body. Scrutinizing the curves, he could not detect anything else. She had surprised him; he didn't want to pay, but there was something about her. He told himself, if he drank lots of her beer it would be just like buying beer.

'Ten dollars US you can stay all afternoon, drink beer, I suck and fuck you, anything you want.' She slipped her small hand into his.

He stepped forward, jerking her arm gently as he did. She anchored her flip-flopped feet, refusing to move.

'You pay first, please.'

He eyed her suspiciously; he didn't need a heat to test if she could swiftly outrun him. He swilled down the dregs of the beer remaining in the can, squeezed it and tossed it into a nearby bush. Still holding her hand, but now with added pressure, he rummaged in his pocket in an attempt to locate a note of the appropriate denomination.

'I'm not going to steal your money,' she said, slightly offended that her morals were being called into question.

'No,' Bulongo replied, extracting a twenty from his trousers and pushing it back down.

'For twenty, I'll let you do it without a condom,' she chirped up in the hope of doubling her take.

Bulongo pulled another note, a second twenty: she didn't look infected. He stuffed it into her hand. Decision taken.

Naked, in a small darkened room of a breeze-block house with many exterior doors, a short walk from the beer hall, she had refused to allow Bulongo to turn on the light. He felt the street-map scald scar on the side of her face she had strategically maintained on the dark side of her client in the daylight, and which he had not seen when he first noticed her working previously. Touching it, he traced it down her neck as it expanded across her small left breast, which conjured up the image of a fried egg. She stepped closer, gently touching their bodies together, but making no movement to remove his hand as he continued to explore her patchwork flesh.

He left as the sun was going down, and feeling he had just spent the best twenty dollars he could remember ever having parted with.

oOo

Jabu had caught the bus, changed, and then caught another. Kunda had arranged for the truck he had travelled on to drop him close to where the long-distance buses picked up and dropped off, overfull and smelling of men that had spent the day working up a sweat to earn sufficient money to support their families. Kunda and Jabu squeezed into a tshova that would take them in the direction of the tsotsi house.

Later, pumping, pounding, the noise, the flashing of lights and the heat were becoming too much. He had danced too much at Jabu's insistence, and his shirt was wringing with sweat. He had drunk more Mosi than he knew he should, and now felt ill. If they went back to the tsotsi house now she would want to fuck. She was buzzing, and if he couldn't she would be flat and bad-mouth him. Bringing her to the city may not have been such a good idea, he thought. Plenty of good-looking women about he could have picked up and dropped as he pleased. He found a corner near the door and collapsed, his head on his knees.

When he woke, the Lusaka sun was shining in through the window. He closed his eyes, trying to take cover in the darkness of the bedclothes. The next time he opened them he did so with caution, using the palm of his hand for added protection. He looked under the sheets which were wet and crumpled in deep, erratic creases; boxers were the only clothes he was wearing. From the room next door, a crowd of laughing people choked off the music, vibrating through the wall, that he had not previously noticed. For a moment he thought he was back in the club, not in bed, not just in his shorts. Crazy. Emerging, he looked around for a suitable missile and, selecting a shoe, hurled it with less power than he would have expected to generate, in a declaration of his need for silence. He fell back onto the mattress and crushed out the noise by clamping a pillow over his head.

Later, a minute or two, an hour or two, he could not be sure, he sensed someone was standing over him. Tentatively, he lifted the pillow; the music penetrated, increasing in volume the greater the gap over his ear became.

'Fuck!' He said it out loud to himself.

'Over here, Bulongo.'

He rolled over and brought a faded print of Christ into focus, then saw a stretched arm and hand holding a Mosi coming into the periphery of his vision. He took the bottle and felt his stomach turn before he could get the neck to his lips.

Jabu slipped under the covers next to him.

'Babbalos bad? They thought a beer would sort your head out better than coffee,' she told him.

The smell of the beer filling his nostrils was being pushed aside by a strong whiff of sex. Honing his memory of the night before, he was unable to recall detail of any action taking place with Jabu. And from what he half-remembered, he could not be certain the images were not merely recollections of a mosaic of the many previous encounters they had enjoyed. The last thing he could truly be certain of before the heat and glare of sun had stirred him, was the moment before he crashed on the bar floor. But then there was the state of the bed linen. He wondered if he had suffered some kind of fit, or a seriously bad dream. Then he realized the smell of alcohol was not emanating from the small uncapped bottle, but from the liquid oozing out from every pore in his body.

'Why do everyone call you Bulongo, Kunda?' she asked, already knowing the meaning of the nickname and knowing that Kunda would also know it was common knowledge.

He looked at her half-smile and wondered if the peal of laughter he had heard in the other room had been at his expense. He didn't need this, the state he was in.

'Because I'm a fighter. When I drive I always fight to get at the front of the line,' he told her.

She leaned over him. He could smell the alcohol on her breath, it wasn't stale or sour. They had been drinking in the other room, starting up again, maybe never stopped.

'Not much of a fighter last night,' she said, slipping her hand into his boxers, but without gaining any response.

oOo

The truck dropped Kunda on the road close to the river. Another hour and it would be dark. Two miles, maybe three, along the river bank, he could see smoke, a thin trail, white before it softly dispersed a few feet above the trees. When he was not tending the garden at the Zimwani, the witch doctor camped out there away from everything, enjoying days of solitude, or in the company of men from the surrounding villages and the less urbanized sorts from the township.

He was tempted. Kunda knew the women at his village

76

would be tight with him, and he was still nursing a babbalos from hell, which the tossing around in the truck had not improved.

He remembered his travel documents pushed deep in his pocket. His visa was multiple-entry, so no problem there considering another alternative; a few days alone on the other side of the river, to get better. All things considered, he turned off the road, looking for a track that would lead him in the direction of the smoke.

As the sun dropped, he was on the only path that could be relied upon, the only one illuminated by the metallic light of the moon mirroring off the water. But it ran too often for Kunda's piece of mind to the very edge, water lapping and washing over his shoes. Twice, a thrashing as his foot splashed down triggered an adrenalin rush, but on both occasions water monitors dived for the safety of the depths, fearful their nests were under threat.

Kunda was beginning to regret he had not returned to the village, but he knew turning around was no solution. Previously unoccupied stretches could not be guaranteed predator-free, even two steps later.

An hour passed and his careful, hesitant strap had not brought him nearer to his destination. From within the trees he was not able to see the smoke, and he could not detect the smell of burning wood. Had it not been for the river, he would have taken a bet that he was strapping round in circles. Fireflies dancing, long dark leaf shadows offering up images of fear, and the cacophony of disturbed birds bursting out did nothing to improve his temperament. He stumbled over protruding roots, with occasional aggressive splashing to his right and crackling of more things he did not wish to contemplate on his left. He stopped, deciding it was as torturous going on as it was stopping to rest. At dawn, he would feel more comfortable, and could make a sensible decision.

'Kunda, come closer. It is not necessary to hide from

me.' The voice was gentle and without menace, but it was sufficient to send a tremble through his entire being. A faint, faint trace on a light breeze, of cooked fish and burnt wood, flecked his nostrils.

'Come through, Kunda, you have nothing to fear.' The invitation came again, and this time without the shock impairing his senses, Kunda was able to recognize the voice of the man he had decided to seek out some three hours earlier.

Carefully, he pushed through the remaining foliage and stepped into a small clearing. Pulled high of the water, a canoe with the name of the lodge painted white in block capitals along the side lay overturned to provide a makeshift platform. As Kunda approached, he could see set out on a white cloth small bunches of hair and, in groups, fine slivers of fingernail trimmings in saucers of dark bark.

The figure seated on a fallen trunk, sat upright, his slender form shrouded in loosely fitting white regalia. In his left hand, stamping his authority, a ceremonial shepherd's crook decorated with silver rings and nibblets. The witch doctor beckoned.

'Do not look so worried Kunda, you have nothing to fear in this world. You may do as you please in the knowledge that your life will be full of pleasure and you will father many sons. Drink some beer, eat some fish, and relax on the edge of the clearing while I sniff out those who would bring evil on other families.'

'How did you know I was here?' Kunda asked.

'You have passed by me three times, but it is only now that I was able to receive you,' the witch doctor explained. 'Now satisfy your thirst and your hunger, while I consider a judgement.'

Kunda wanted to leave, he didn't know why, but could not bring himself to turn around. The fire burned hot, he could feel the heat through the material of his trousers as he approached the pit. Behind it, a few feet away, a large crumpled sheet of aluminium foil protected a substantial tigerfish from still-glowing embers where it had cooked at the side of the main flames. The top fillet had already been pulled away from behind the head. Kunda cautiously picked flesh from above the tail in the hope that the cage of fine bones, difficult to see in the poor light, could be avoided. Using an A10 peach can, the only container he could see, Kunda scooped milky liquid from a large blackened kettle in which the substance had been boiled and re-boiled, although now it was as cool as the air temperature would permit. Drinking carefully from the sharp, jagged edge, through gritted teeth, he filtered lumps that in the village he would have swallowed without a thought. Out here chibuku brewed by a witch doctor, everyone knew, could well contain dead animals or even stillborn infants, in the belief it adds potency to the concoction.

Rightly or wrongly, he estimated the can held two pints. By the time the river began to turn orange just before sunrise, he had returned to the kettle twice more, tripping over uneven ground on the last occasion. Had it not been for the ribbing pressed into the metal, the can and the beer would have been lost from his grasp.

The witch doctor had not spoken to him since their first exchange on his arrival, despite Kunda attempting a quiet address on his way to the kettle. Sniffing, constant sniffing; and then a gentle chant in words Kunda could not make out. Now, with the sun replacing the moon, straight-backed, staffed hand still unrelenting, he sat, perfectly still, perfectly silent.

When he woke, the tin lay next to him on its side, empty. The morning rays glinted off it, flashing in Kunda's eyes, adding to the burning sensation he was experiencing. His mouth tasted vile and when he struggled to stand, his legs buckled and his head swam. The clear ground where he had fallen was only slightly bigger than his own mass, the landscape around him seemed to be breathing, sweating. He recalled walking, but couldn't bring himself to trust his intuition. His head spinning. Dancing, lights, music, women, people, but this did not seem to fit in with his whereabouts now. That had all been before. Walking. Walking in straight lines, walking round about. Walking into a clearing. But then something vague, wandering away, loomed. His nails scratched small lumps on his skin. His ankles and then his neck itched. Scratching close to his face, he could see that his nails had been cut. He tried to take stock of his surroundings.

Loud reports from large-calibre rifles echoed around him. He guessed at poachers locating elephant or rhino on the other side of the river. Followed up quickly by multiple bursts of semi-automatic weapons, it probably meant the poachers had run into an Anti-Poaching Unit and were caught up in a fire-fight. The sounds echoed, buffeting his ears. He realized he could not be sure where he was in relation to the river, or how far he had strayed from the clearing. He had assumed he had been unconscious for one full day, but now he knew this was without any foundation. He looked for his bag, which he could not find, but was sure he would have been carrying one when he was dropped from the truck. Vomit exploded from his mouth and acid cut his sinuses. 'Fuck, fuck, fuck!' he wailed, but the words were not strong enough to make a sound, as white foaming liquid won the cavity of his mouth and his stomach began to spasm for the third time.

CHAPTER EIGHT

Since moving into the flat above the office, Romance felt
her position at the company was changing. It wasn't
anything that anyone had said, it was underpinned as much
by the way she was treated, particularly by the teams of men
who now seemed to ask her where previously they would
have informed her. Although the walk to work had always
been short, plus having use of all the labour-saving devices,
she seemed to be at her desk much earlier and, although not
consciously, she stayed longer after the office had closed;
accepting enquiries from clients who phoned late or tried
the door after office hours.

Mr Stephen had announced that Romance and Kingsley
would join him for lunch each Friday, that he had enjoyed
their lunch together previously, and that it would be a good
opportunity to have their weekly planning meeting in a
more convivial environment. This had now become
routine. The lodges were reporting many bookings from
new agents located in areas where the safari interest had
never before been significant, and this was reflected in the
increase in Romance and Kingsley's workload. The figures
Kingsley had presented at their last working lunch
prompted Mr Stephen to plan another trip up to the north

of the country, even more determined to establish a presence there. He decided that Romance should make his travel arrangements for the end of the month, which was three weeks away. In his absence, Kingsley would be in charge of all the accounting and finance, while Romance would take full control of operations. Not a new situation, but the first time it would be formalized with the circulation of a memo.

'You must be very confident,' Kingsley had told her, when they returned to the office after lunch. 'Some of the men in the teams will not be happy taking direct orders from a woman,' he added, a sincere concern in his voice.

'It is no more or no less than is always the case,' she assured him, knowing well that Mr Stephen putting her new status in writing was a significant step that a few of the older men in the teams would baulk against. But deep inside she felt this was a move up that she wanted and she could feel the swell of determination gathering inside her to succeed. Later, on her own after everyone had left and all was locked up, she carried out role play, sitting at Mr Stephen's desk, discussing new installations with imaginary clients and making calls to slack suppliers demanding they provide a better service or risk losing her business. Someone would be needed to run the new office if Mr Stephen's ambitions proved successful, and it was close to an area she knew. She would make Kunda so proud, and then they would not have to be apart. She could live at home and commute.

'Did your man love you in your new dress?' the woman asked, rising up from a squatting position behind her stall, which was stacked high with neatly folded clothing. 'He has sent you to me to buy one or two more?' she asked, hoping to sell another expensive garment.

'He has not seen it.' Romance responded with undisguised sadness in her voice.

'I cannot give you a refund or buy it back for the money

you paid,' the stall owner butted in, fearful she was about to face losing her most expensive sale, pointing to a hand-scrawled sign pinned to an upright, supporting her stance.

'No. He had to work, so he couldn't visit. But he will see me in it soon. He's promised to come to me when he gets some time off. A few weeks, maybe sooner,' she said, wishing to put the woman's mind at ease.

'Then what do you want?' the woman asked suspiciously.

'Something smart. A suit,' Romance said, casting her glance over the merchandise to see if anything stood out.

'You have to go to court? You've been a bad girl?' the woman asked, sneering at the idea someone like Romance could have any other reason for acquiring such an outfit.

'It's for the office. I have recently been promoted,' she retorted, holding her head up, with an overwhelming desire to physically look down on the vendor, if only her stature had truly permitted. 'Two. I am looking for two. Maybe you don't have anything smart like that,' she added cattily.

Sitting in her room, the TV chatting in the corner, Romance was undecided whether to wear her new outfit before Mr Stephen left on his travels, or to wait until after he had gone. She thought about it while viewing herself in the mirror. She looked at herself critically, now worried she had spent money outside her budget. The memo that Mr Stephen had said he would send out did not change her job title, and there had certainly been no offer of extra money for the added responsibility. She now felt she had been stupid. Kunda would be angry at the cost of the clothes, which she had finally bought from the store on the main street, not having found anything suitable on the stall. And the staff would laugh at her imagining she was anything but the girl who worked in the office. She removed the jacket and skirt and laid them on the bed, smoothing out the creases before folding them back into the plastic bag with the shop's name emblazoned in green across the side. It should go back, she decided. Then she sat in the middle of the bed and sobbed at her own ridiculousness.

In the office the following day, her glumness lifted when a boy delivered her a folded envelope. The lined paper inside, torn from an exercise book, had a few words written by Kunda, telling the dates he was expecting to be off and when she should be at the bus station to meet him. She visualized searching for his face as the passengers queued to alight from the bus. It had been months. Then she saw him and smiled, and the longing she felt was real. But as the thought gave her pleasure, it also nudged her memory of Sonkwe delivering the last letter she had received from her sister. Had she not written again, had she been resigned to using the post, notorious for loss and delivery times that exceeded a calculation of time itself … Should she have been a little more relaxed with Sonkwe for the sake of her sister? A light kiss maybe, the undeclared possibility of more when the messenger returned. The thought of even him contemplating her in that way repulsed her; made her skin pimple. She pledged, if no word came before she was due time off, she would travel south to see her sister and spend a few days with her.

Kingsley brought a file to her, with the suggestion that if the company were to undertake any further work for the client in question, payment should be obtained before work was commenced.

'He's a very small client and he continually ignores requests for settlement of his account. I spend more time trying to extract payment than the value of his business.' Romance said she would flag his account on the computer. She also elaborated on her happiness that she would soon be seeing Kunda and the sadness she felt for her sister, in reply to his enquiry as to her earlier joy and then a cloud of dejection. Kingsley beamed her a grin and told her he was pleased her husband would be visiting soon, and added that the silence from her sister was no doubt as she suspected, due to the unreliability of the postal service. She did not mention her doubts and apprehension concerning her position while Mr Stephen was away.

Telephone enquiries, completed triplicate order forms returned, signed delivery notes, work schedules and remittance cheques seemed in Romance's recollection to be double that of the previous year. Methodically she dealt with each, stapling together those sheets destined for the teams in the yard, in the full knowledge that unsecured batches of paper would result in pages being lost or mislaid, in turn causing jobs to be partially completed, followed by phone calls from irate clients. Kingsley's batches she collated using paper clips as each sheet, having been logged and reconciled, would be filed individually in meticulous order in separate lever-arch files. Cheques she entered in a special 'cheques received' book which she had drawn up with pencilled columns setting out all the relevant details before passing those over to Kingsley to prepare for Mr Stephen to bank. It was all part of the intricate system that Mr Robertson had set up, and in which she had been instructed on her first day. Kingsley had thanked her shortly after she had started for the care she obviously took in marshalling the paperwork, before passing it over, and he was regularly complimentary. The care needed was not insignificant and she knew a person less meticulous, with the increased volumes the business was experiencing, would have left each department to sort themselves out. But that was not her way, and the increased industry assisted her to put some insecurities out of her head.

Planning out Mr Stephen's travel schedule, it appeared likely Kunda's visit would coincide with Mr Stephen's business trip. She realized taking time off to spend with her husband would be impossible. But if she neglected Kunda, she was worried that he would be angry with her. Putting him off was also something she felt unable to even consider. Romance decided that it was stupid to speculate on her quandary; it may be that the programme Mr Stephen was expecting could not be achieved, accommodation might be full, seats on the plane might not be available, and prospective clients might be away on business.

'Kingsley, I'm going upstairs for my lunch and then I'm going to walk to Travel Mart to arrange Mr Stephen's bookings,' she said coming out from behind her desk, sliding typed sheets of the schedule into a clear blue plastic envelope.

'Book a trip to London while you're there. I could use a break,' he replied, smiling and pointing to the stack of files on his desk and the taller pile on the floor beside it.

Romance smiled at his joke. 'Business Class?'

'No, first I think, Business will remind me too much of all this.'

'First it is then,' she assured him.

'What is first? Something I should know about?' Mr Stephen asked, coming back in from completing a site visit.

Romance explained the joke.

'I think Cape Town would be more enticing. When I spoke to my parents last week they said the whole of Britain was freezing and snow was forecast. Bad weather in spring seems to be becoming a regular occurrence.'

'Either would be only a dream at the moment. It is difficult enough to find time even for lunch,' Kingsley said without concern.

'Maybe we should consider employing an office assistant, if business continues to improve. It's something we could discuss over lunch tomorrow,' Mr Stephen suggested.

Romance unconsciously bit her lip, worried this suggestion may be a reflection on her position. After all, when she had been first employed, 'office assistant' had been the advertisement to which she had replied.

After she had eaten some sadza, with a little relish she had retained from her meal the previous day, she went back downstairs. Kingsley had left to purchase a snack from the vendor across the street, which allowed him to be absent from his desk for the shortest possible time.

'Romance, can you come into the office for a moment, please.' Mr Stephen was sitting behind his desk when Romance entered. He withdrew a key from his pocket and, pushing himself on the castors of his high-backed chair, opened the small safe that was bolted to the floor behind him. Over his shoulder, craning her neck, Romance could just make out her two envelopes of savings where she had placed them with her own hand, after her last pay-day. Was Mr Stephen going to hand them to her and explain that her services were no longer required; that the company needed to employ someone who could work harder and assist Kingsley in keeping his workload down?

'I think they may ask you for this before they can book the plane ticket.' Mr Stephen turned and smiled, holding out his deep-red British passport for Romance to take.

The town was quite busy, there was a sense of industry not forced. A pent-up exuberance released. It gave her a good feeling. Children, too young for school, were playing on the pavement outside shops, while mothers inside filled their lists. Bakkies with lodge insignias were being loaded outside the hardware store, jerry cans were being topped up for camps located on the islands where power relied upon generators run for restricted periods, and council employees wearing suits and carrying briefcases or clipboards headed to and from the Town Hall. As she walked, she could hear familiar music, but could not completely bring to mind the song. Romance watched Kingsley, sat in the window concentrating on his food and a lemonade drink, unaware of Romance as she strolled purposefully by, enjoying the warmth of the afternoon sun on her body. The sound grew louder as she approached a record shop, where the owner sat outside, his chair leaning back against the wall while he lounged, waiting for customers. By the time she drew level, the track had ended and another which she had not heard before took over. Two more blocks, and she arrived at the Travel Mart, it's shop-front windows plastered with A4 sheets, offers rainbow-written in different coloured felt tip, for cheap flights to popular destinations around the world, cheap travel insurance, dollar, rand, sterling exchange rates, *The best in town – no commission*, safari trips locally and in all six neighbouring countries, extreme sports bookings and baggage repository. Romance pushed open the door to be greeted with the whirl of fans, and the welcome respite of cool air.

'I wish to book a flight for Mr Simons of Krystaal Pool Supplies, and a hire car,' Romance said as she advanced across the dimly lit room to the counter on the far side.

The woman who remained largely hidden behind a computer screen made little effort towards acknowledgement. Romance found and plumped down in a red, plastic bucket chair opposite, and waited patiently. After five minutes of being ignored, she coughed gently. The deeply tanned woman, who Romance calculated was at least a couple of years younger than herself, leaned round the barrier that was between them.

'I'll be with you shortly. I just want to finish this email.' The statement, in a strong Australian accent, was without emotion, neither irritated nor with any sign of consideration. A simple matter of complete disinterest.

'Excuse me, but I do have to get back to the office, and this is quite important.' Romance spoke out after a further extended period of silence, during which no effort to attend to her was forthcoming.

'What was it you wanted?' the Aussie girl asked, with one eye still monitoring her screen.

'I wish to book a flight to the north for my boss.' Romance spoke with an abruptness that would have been greater had she not been worried her attitude would be considered antagonistic. She could not afford to be detained away from the office for the entire afternoon.

The Aussie girl pushed her chair away from the desk so that the top of her body was now fully visible, and then stretched, pushing her bra-less breasts forward.

'I just deal with the extreme sports,' she informed Romance, pointing at the logo and picture of Victoria Falls bridge with a bungee-jumper in full flight, before scooting back out of view. 'Mr Khan, someone here wants to book a flight or something,' she added in a slightly raised voice to no one Romance could locate.

'I'll be there in a moment, tell them.' A tinny voice from somewhere in the building crackled through the speaker of an intercom Romance tracked down to a dusty pale-green plastic contraption the size of a cigarette box hanging from a nail on the wall.

The Aussie girl made no attempt to pass on the message, no doubt assuming Romance had heard. But Romance supposed it was equally likely she didn't care one way or the other.

After five minutes a very tall woman, wearing a peach-coloured sari, appeared from a doorway behind the counter.

'What is it you want? Mr Khan is still busy,' she asked, walking past Romance to a computer at the other end of the counter.

'A flight, and to book a hire car,' Romance replied, turning her chair to face in the new direction.

'Would you sit down here, please?'

Romance moved the few feet and deposited herself on an identical chair opposite the woman who now appeared to be dealing with her requirement.

'The system has been down for a couple of hours, but I'll see what we can do.'

Romance explained that she was in a hurry now, as she had already been kept waiting for twenty minutes.

'I'm sorry, but the seat you were sitting in is for extreme sports. If you had sat here in the beginning Mr Khan would have seen you and come straight down,' she explained, pointing to a small CCTV camera mounted on a chipped grey metal filing cabinet in an alcove behind her.

Romance finally arrived back in her office a little before four, in a state of clear irritation.

'I thought you'd booked the ticket to London and left,' Stephen joked when she relayed her experience in Travel Mart.

'If we ran our business like that there would be no business,' Romance complained.

'You should have gone to the travel desk in the hotel,' Kingsley told her, 'They're pretty switched on. Travel Mart is mainly for backpackers,' he added with an uncharacteristic note of contempt, as he wiped a fine bead of sweat from his forehead.

Stephen had noticed his bookkeeper looked out of sorts earlier in the day, and taking account of the stack of files beside his desk, which didn't seem to be shrinking, he had earlier in the day rescheduled their weekly lunch to Monday.

'You seem to be flagging fast,' Stephen said as Kingsley pushed his chair back from the desk and arched his aching back.

'I'm OK,' Kingsley assured him as he repositioned himself and opened a new file. 'I don't think the aircon is working too well.'

'You could be right,' Stephen agreed. 'It's Friday afternoon and the end of a hell of a week. I think you could call it a day and I'll see if I can get one of the guys in on Saturday to test the system.' Stephen could see his suggestion was an appreciated thought, despite Kingsley's protests.

'Take the rest of the afternoon off and come in on Monday, bright and fresh. I'm sure then you'll fly through that lot. No point sitting there forcing your brain to work.'

'Well, if you are sure Stephen, but I will take some work home with me. There are five or six files I will need you to look at before you go up north,' Kingsley said, turning to the extent of the work required as he spoke.

Romance returned to her desk resolved to work late, with the added possibility of coming down over the weekend. The last thing she wanted was to be taking decisions on more things than was necessary, and she knew that on Monday, with picking up the tickets and making all the other arrangements for Mr Stephen's trip, everything would take longer than she could afford.

Kingsley called goodbye as he left with a mountain of files cradled close to his chest.

o0o

When Romance returned to the office on Monday morning, the wall clock ticked to 10.30 as she entered. The collection of the tickets had been more speedy than she had expected, but still longer than she had hoped. The office was unmanned and this was always her concern if she was away from her desk for any period of time. Kingsley could not be expected to remain at his desk regardless, and she knew it was sure to be one of those occasions when he was out of the room that a customer would come in. And then there was the security implication that bothered her as much, if not more. Maybe the idea of an office assistant could be defended. Certainly, Kingsley's desk did not show signs of his workload being diminished.

Having first waited a few minutes, listening to make sure he wasn't with a client or talking privately on the telephone, Romance knocked gently on Mr Stephen's door, which unusually, along with the window blinds, was closed.

'Come in.'

Stephen was sitting behind his desk and, as far as Romance could make out when she entered, he seemed to be in the middle of nothing. She wondered if he might have been dozing when she knocked.

'I have your schedule, tickets, car rental documents – you will need to be sure to have your driving licence with you when you go to collect the car,' she told him with a smile, to reassure him that she was confident all had been prepared correctly.

'Kingsley is dead,' he told her, in a monotone devoid of expression and without shifting his position. He seemed to be in a state of shock.

'His wife phoned and asked for me to send her money.' He didn't move. 'To buy firewood,' he added by way of an explanation in a statement that he did not understand.

'How?' she asked

'Malaria. She said he arrived home feeling unwell on Friday, it went cerebral on Sunday morning and he died in the evening.'

'I think he was a good man. We will need to look hard to find a replacement,' she said, placing the folder of travel documents in front of Stephen. Her concerns were drawn to the desk outside where the files would remain, more would be added and, if action was not urgently taken, could cause the business to grind to a standstill.

'Should we not ...' Stephen's words tailed off, unsure of how to word the ending. Then he did it again.

'Romance, you don't seem ...,' he said now, looking at her in the face, frowning and trying to judge her emotions.

'We are resigned to death in this country, Mr Stephen. Every week people hear of someone dying. AIDS, malaria, road accidents. In the villages you will find there are not many over the age of fifty. They say in this country even the elders are young. I will miss Kingsley, I liked him and I am sad that he has died. But I must get on and live my life,' she explained, realizing that Europeans, in her knowledge, reacted differently. It was not easy pushing emotion deep. But she knew herself, either it would be held down with the weight of a heavy stone, or erupt beyond control. *You or I could be next*, she did not say. But she felt this, and took control.

Romance ate a sandwich in the office, which she had made quickly upstairs. She had been able to complete most of her work by giving up most of the weekend to it. Being in this position pleased her. She decided to look at Kingsley's work during the afternoon, but was worried she would not be able to make head or tail of it. She would ask Mr Stephen's permission to approach the headmistress at the local grammar school to see if any of the students, soon to finish their studies, could be recommended for the position of office assistant.

'I don't understand why Kingsley's wife has asked for money to buy firewood,' Stephen said, standing behind her while she made a list of each client file on Kingsley's desk, trying to understand the difference in the processing of those selected for the stack on the floor.

'It is the union agreement that employers pay for the firewood and the hire of the trucks,' she explained.

Stephen contemplated the reply.

'I don't understand,' he said, trying to imagine a reason for such a strange union perk.

Romance could see the retained confusion in Mr Stephen's brow.

'When a member of the family dies, the family have to provide the firewood for the crematorium and pay the cost of hiring a truck to transport the coffin and the mourners. If two or three members of the same family die in one year, the cost can cause great hardship,' she explained. 'If it is the breadwinner, the family may be left destitute. Many very old people who have been lucky to survive so long are burying their children and their grandchildren. Things have swung from one direction to another in this country, in much of Africa. Once people died before they got old, of poor food, a lack of simple medical care, clean water. Now AIDS is the big killer, taking our young men and women. Many babies die from malaria and are HIV-positive when they are born.'

It was only now that Stephen realized the significance of the open trucks he had seen regularly on the road leading to the edge of town. The loads of people, crowded on board, some sitting on top of the cab, were not gangs of workers being transported to and from the fields, but friends and relations of the dead. The tall chimney in the distance could be seen to release smoke flecked with ash almost constantly during daylight hours.

The following day when he arrived at the office, an envelope had been delivered by hand. He removed the single typed sheet of paper.

BURIAL PROGRAMME FOR THE LATE:

MR. KINGSLEY GABUZA

TIME	WHAT TO DO
13.30	Gathering at the Mortuary
14.00	Leave the mortuary for the Crematorium
14.30	Church Service
15.00	Cremation of the Body
15.15	Laying of Wreaths
15.30	Speech from Church Leader
	Speech from the Employer
	Speech from Relatives
	End of Programme

Note:
Body viewing will only be done at the mortuary before it is put in the coffin.
Note:
The wake will be held at the home of the deceased's parents.

Romance had taken Kingsley's advice and gone to the

travel desk in the hotel to change Stephen's bookings. When she returned, she gave the new tickets to Stephen and advised him on local tradition.

'You should wear old clothes and old shoes if you have them; it is the custom,' she told him.

Stephen closed the office, drove himself and Romance to the service on the day Kingsley's body was to be offered up to his maker, and permitted the work teams to use the company vehicles to attend.

Romance wore a washed-out chitenge wrapped tightly round her waist down to the flip-flops on her feet, and had her hair pulled in a state of disarray in the traditional way for such an occasion.

It was a Christian affair, which Chipo had not fought against when Kingsley's father, who had never truly approved of his son's conversion to a faith he did not recognize, took on all responsibility.

More trucks arrived outside the cement-block building before the formalities were finished. Stephen could feel the pressure to vacate. Those other groups, also seeking to release their dead and resume a life less full, milled around on the dried, well-walked grass where they themselves had earlier lingered anxiously before being ushered in.

During the cremation, the women's wailing was loud and high-pitched; the men lamented with their deep-toned kukhuza. Chipo was comforted by the women close to her family. She was gaunt and grief-stricken, her head shaved, her gaze absent.

Some of the speeches conveyed deep sorrow, bringing further crying and wailing; some included amusing anecdotes causing reflective smiles but little laughter. When it came to Stephen's turn, he kept his speech short, saying he had not known Kingsley long but during the time they had been acquainted he had come to know Kingsley as a good man, a hard and conscientious worker who could be relied upon. An extremely sad loss to the business, his colleagues and family.

At the wake, unlike their celebratory gathering at the same venue a few weeks earlier, most guests gravitated to the rear of the house, rather than to the front. Some stood looking thoughtfully out across the river, which had subsided to within the defines of the banks, increasing the size of the garden substantially. Others chatted in groups, not wishing to contemplate any similarities with the determination of their own fate. Stephen remained outside with the majority of men whilst the women congregated mainly in the house, as was the convention. Romance stood alone watching a fish eagle perched in a tree. Motionless, it scrutinized the river surface for signs of life to scoop up in its featherless talons, and fly high in the blue sky to feed eager beaks.

Pleased to have located her, Stephen offered a glass of cold liquid he had brought from the kitchen, which she took, muttering a quiet toast before taking a sip.

'To life,' Stephen repeated.

After an hour they took their leave, shaking hands with members of Kingsley's family, on their way to the front gate, and with Sanjay Johal, who was quietly circulating among the more affluent of the mourners. All spoke of Kingsley's good nature and diligence, and offered condolences were offered once more. As they left, the fish eagle had forsaken its perch and flown low over the water, snatching its prize before gaining height.

'His family will feed well tonight,' Stephen commented, as he shaded his eyes to keep the bird in sight.

'And another family will have lost a relative,' Romance said.

Stephen wasn't sure that fish actually operated a family unit, but he understood the sentiment and so refrained from comment.

On the drive back, Stephen was surprised to find that

Romance seemed to be of the opinion few of her countrymen had any interest in the wildlife, and that it was only recently they had been persuaded it wasn't in their interest to kill as much of the game as possible. How this equated with the fish family loss he was not sure.

'The elephants trample the crops and feed on the corn, the cattle are killed and eaten by wild beasts, and the chickens are taken by the hunting birds. Even young childrens' lives are put at risk. I remember my grandfather saying that if the white people wanted to save all the animals they should take them back to their country and let them loose there.'

Stephen laughed.

'Tourism is a big employer, and it's an industry that will grow. It provides work,' Stephen argued, not wishing to personalize it too much by referring to their pool business.

'Stephen, we were a nation of farmers. Many do not want to leave the land to make beds, clean toilets and serve food every day, food they could afford maybe only once a year.' She wanted to explain more. She had suddenly felt more than she had previously understood, but at that moment they arrived back outside the office, and the mountain of work that was stacked up behind the door pushed the new thoughts back into the recesses where they had previously nestled dormant.

Three days later, Stephen withdrew money from the petty cash tin, replacing it with the requisite slip, for the provision of a second load of firewood.

CHAPTER NINE

'When will you be back?' Jabu asked, sulking at the prospect of her husband and her lover both being away at the same time.

He had entered her on one of the two day-beds in the fishing shack they had been sent to prepare for guests soon to arrive with a fishing guide. It had been over too quick. But the clean linen and the cold boxes, containing the guests' food and drink, were still in the bakkie, and neither had wanted to be caught.

'Four days,' he said, humping the container filled with bottles of Heineken and ice through the narrow door.

'Four days is too long,' she pouted.

He had come on the mattress, and she could smell their sex. She turned it and opened the windows, then used the scent of the mosquito spray as camouflage before they left. She wanted him to stop on the drive back and make love to her properly, to finish the urge that had been left incomplete. Bulongo pushed her hand away from his crotch and changed gear before accelerating out onto the tarmac road.

'Are you saving yourself for that stupid wife of yours?' she said, more as an accusation than a question.

'If I don't hurry, I'll miss the bus. I didn't think I'd have to drive all the way out here this morning. *Duzvi*, I should have been finished straight after breakfast.' The irritation in his voice swirled.

He pulled out to overtake a truck travelling south from Zaire, and had to swerve at the last moment on the wrong side of the road to avoid a pothole.

'Fuck the Minister for Roads. He will not be happy until we're all dead,' Bulongo cursed.

Jabu did not reply. She did not see how it was the Minister's fault that the trucks, the sun and the rain caused the roads to break up. After sitting in silence for ten minutes and still staring out of the passenger window at the rubbish blowing across the land that was already showing signs of drying out, Jabu spoke softly.

'You could drive – you don't have to catch the bus.'

'If Romance sees the condition of the car she will not speak to me anymore,' he replied, annoyed at the thought of the idea.

'She won't let you fuck her, you mean,' she said, looking at him now.

He turned to see the anger in her face, but she was smiling. He realized she was laughing at him.

o0o

The bus bounced more than the car or the bakkie, and harder, as though the tyres were solid. The passengers lifted and fell back over each pothole, and trembled above their seats when a strip of the road underneath had crumbled away in long tracks from one edge to the other side. Hands grabbed the nearest solid part of the interior, and the sound echoed around like a burst of automatic fire. Trucks pounded down behind them, horns blaring, in constant demand for the bus to pull over, regardless that to do so would send it off the road across dust and rubble.

Tailgating was routine until the opportunity to overtake presented itself, often leaving only inches of free space between the two vehicles as they passed. The vacuum this created held the bus taut down its complete length, and only when a truck eventually took the lead could both the bus and its passengers feel the release of its invisible force.

At the first few stops, more people got on than off. Most were not carrying bags for long journeys, so he thought they were simply travelling between villages. The young woman who had climbed into the seat two rows ahead of Kunda, after the second stop, was the only redemption of his choice of transport. Her hair had been straightened and, from the angle of his view, Kunda could see the swell of her breasts each time the bus hovered above the road. But this pleasure was fleeting as a backpacker took the seat just ahead of him. Balancing his bag on his lap, the foreigner leaned forward and used it as a hard cushion to support his prospect of sleep.

Kunda was tired, but he could not understand how anyone sober could even doze in such uncomfortable surroundings.

The next stop was at a small village set back off the road. Thatches could be seen pointing above the sparse tree line. Four passengers stood and manoeuvred their way along the aisle as the engine shuddered and the brakes screeched the bus to a standstill. The backpacker had slumped with his shoulder protruding and half-woke, mumbling as he was pushed aside to make way.

No one got on. And across the aisle from the young woman, who had been obscured from Kunda's view and was his only source of pleasure, a seat had been vacated. The bus pulled away and those who had alighted hurried towards the village, along the narrow path worn in the grass, to escape the cloud of dust generated by the wheels. Kunda changed his seat.

At the next stop, which did not seem to have the

justification of even a few thatched dwellings or passenger movement, the young woman, having politely ignored Kunda's attempts at conversation, moved to the seat he had previously occupied. And, before he could gather his thoughts, the backpacker had sprung from his catatonic state into the freed space, stretching himself across both seats. The bus did not stop again for more than an hour. When it did, it was at a small town spreading out from where the main road took a sharp turn to the left.

The young woman, the backpacker, and more than half of the remaining passengers left the bus. Those with luggage waited for the driver to unlash the cases and pass them down from the roof.

'We're here for an hour, and there won't be another stop after this for many miles,' the driver shouted in to the passengers who had remained in their seats, before he wandered off, returning a few minutes later with a bucket of fried chicken from a nearby fast-food store.

An old man poked Kunda in the shoulder with a finger that looked too podgy for his spindly arms and body, and stood up waiting for Kunda to allow him to leave his seat. Kunda did not stand: he swung his legs into the aisle, which he decided provided a broad enough path.

'Keep it for me. I'm coming back,' The old man said, and pushed past.

The smell of the driver's lunch reminded Kunda how hungry he felt. The hollowness in the base of his stomach ceased to be an occasional rumble and had turned into a hard pain. The temptation to buy food and hang the cost was not easy to put aside, but he did not want to meet Romance with no money in his pocket. The cost of a meal was not a great deal, but it did represent a significant amount of the money he was carrying. Kunda had not received Romance's savings since before Christmas, so with that waiting to fill his wallet he was not worried about having insufficient smeka to give her a good time during his visit.

He left the bus and urinated at the side of the road. The ache he had felt seemed to diminish as he emptied his bladder and he returned to the bus without having spent on food. Other people were starting to rejoin, picking their seats and putting their belongings down next to them in the hope that it would discourage others from choosing to sit beside them. The aroma of lunch and the crackle of food packaging hung in the air, doused by the shuffling of feet and the strong smell of sweat.

Kunda sat where the backpacker had been, and did not remark when a new passenger occupied the old man's place.

The back of his leg above his knee was numb from the seat's metal rim pushing up and through the material, interrupting his circulation. He moved his foot for the needles and pins to dance around. He wanted to walk up and down the aisle, which a number of other suffering passengers had done at various intervals, but his shoe had landed on an object and to walk away risked the near-certainty of it sliding further past him, or back along the floor. The man sitting in the next seat was eyeing him with annoyance as he continued to gyrate his lower body in an attempt to regain feeling without the loss of his booty; the contents of which he was keen to explore.

At the next stop, the one before his, and the bus's terminus, the man stood to leave, and waited for Kunda to stand aside. Even turning to make room he knew would require giving up the hold he had maintained with some discomfort for what he imagined was not less than forty miles. The man, impatient, waved the back of his palm in a gesture to move, for fear the bus would leave with him still on board.

The driver, for reasons that were not to clear to Kunda or any of the other passengers, shunted the vehicle forward no more than a foot. A sound of surprise rose from the passengers and those, including the man next to Kunda, who were not holding on or sat squarely back, were caught off-balance. Kunda was given the opportunity, which he exploited, to instigate some fancy footwork and send the secured square object into a pile of screwed-up cartons the man had discarded on the floor.

Kunda stood and stepped aside, immediately taking the man's seat as he lumbered to alight. Before bending down, Kunda waited until the bus had moved off and everyone had settled back for the final leg of the trip.

Ketchup smeared parts of the outside where it had been in contact with the French-fries cone. Kunda discreetly wiped it and his hands on the underside of the seat, and then, using his body as cover, opened the wallet.

Had he been heading for the capital or across to Lusaka, the three credit cards and driving licence he could have sold for good money. He flicked through the notes, a bunch of Zim dollars, a few Zambian Kwacha, ten SA rand and a fifty-dollar US. 'Lekker,' he whispered under his breath, using South African slang. Feeling great, he slipped the notes into his pocket, closed the wallet and dropped it back into the lunch garbage. Had he been more thorough, his gratification would have been massive. Slipped into the cut lining were two five-hundred-dollar bills, crisp, folded and ironed. Enough for a flight back to the US. But that luck, he missed.

As he left the bus he kicked the bundle hard using the back of his heel, sending it skidding towards the rear.

CHAPTER TEN

Romance began to dress, admiring the underwear she had purchased at the same time as her party dress, but until now had not taken from its bag. Even on her overly rounded body she had to admit it looked good. She looked good. She looked at the plastic clock, next to her bed made with clean, pressed sheets. An hour, and the bus from home would finally be arriving, with Kunda on board. She should have been happy, but she had felt a wave of sadness, nursing a heavy heart, attempting to put the tragedies that life dealt to one side.

Pulling the crotch of her panties to one side, she lowered herself onto his hardness. Her demanding everything he could give, him taking what she had to offer.

They had hurried straight from the bus station back to her flat. It had been many months, too many months, since she had felt a man, her man, inside her. And it was not until they were alone, naked next to each other, that she realized how much she had missed the man she loved making love to her.

Now he lay there, his chest rising and falling, as he slept. Romance watched him, examining the marks and blemishes, the imperfections. He opened his eyes once and caught her looking, but did not speak. He seemed startled, curious, but still did not speak. Then he closed his eyes and fell into a heavier unconsciousness.

She tried to analyse his face, she ran her fingers over the burn scars on his hands and wrists, where he had come into contact with hot plates and sharp knives as he went about his employment. She used her foot, which she had to stretch, to edge his feet apart. They were feet that worked hard, further casualties to his trade. Dress shoes that were too tight and gave little. Buying cheap footwear was a false economy; she would persuade him to buy better, not to be so harsh in his determination to save. She touched his cheek with the back of her hand and smiled.

The evening before, she had cleaned the flat thoroughly, and now she could see there was already a cobweb in the corner above the door. Trapped, she watched a small moth making an impossible effort to extricate itself. The thought of premature death saddened her. She had not heard from her sister since Sonkwe's last delivery, a good few months back. She wondered if Prudence was now dead, but the thought she would not have been sent word seemed unlikely.

She brushed a tear that had slipped from her eye. She wanted Kunda to wake, so they could make love again, or go out, but she did not want to disturb him.

Gently she slipped from the bed, put on a housecoat and quietly went through to the living room. The work had already started to pile up, even before she had started to prepare for Kunda's arrival. At her kitchen table she opened a file she had brought from downstairs, deciding to take advantage of Kunda's slumber. But her mind was not on the requirements of the business. She could not put the silence from her sister to one side. Ridiculously, she was distracted by the patter patter of the tiny wings in the web, and visualized the thrashing of the small feet in the air, not knowing if the feet even existed. At the moment of Kingsley's death, did he know or even guess, Romance wondered.

She sat sipping a cold soda with the file on the table, closed.

Stephen had asked her, as he was writing out the cheque to cover the purchase of the second supply of firewood, but she had been unable to tell him, too ashamed. It had not been a conversation she had been prepared to enter into. She pushed the thought from her mind only to have the space filled with more of the same. She recalled a conversation in the office not long after she had joined the company. The body of an old man had been found in the bush. It was believed he had not wanted to be a burden on his family, so he had walked away into the wilderness, until death had overtaken him. Stephen had likened it to the action of ageing elephants who could no longer feed themselves and would leave the herd to die. Kingsley had told Stephen that people were not animals, and that Mohammad had said *he that throttled himself would be throttled forever in the Fire and he that stabbed himself would be forever stabbed in Hell.*

'The man that had walked to starvation would surely wander starving for all eternity,' Kingsley had added.

Maybe she had remembered wrong; she thought she also remembered Kingsley constantly saying that Allah was all merciful and all compassionate. Romance tried to evoke a sermon she had heard in church, but concluded it was a subject her priest had not broached.

When Kunda awoke, they neither made love nor went out. Kunda showered and wandered around the flat with a towel wrapped around his waist. Romance watched him as she cooked; he looked uneasy, as though he was searching; looking to find meaning rather than any particular object, seeking understanding.

From the supermarket she had purchased beef; she

could not remember when previously she had spent money on red meat. Now she fried it in a little oil and added chopped chillies, grated ginger, crushed garlic and fresh herbs she had chopped that morning and kept in the fridge. On her trip to the supermarket, she had also bought a case of beer for Kunda to drink, having persuaded one of the yard men to ferry her and her heavy groceries back. She opened a bottle and poured half the liquid into a glass, and the remainder she poured into her cooking pan and added quarters of peeled potatoes, another ingredient she rarely cooked for herself.

Kunda ate the food without comment. He smoked a little weed, which Romance had refused, but she had not scolded him. She was a little disappointed he had ignored the dish she had specially prepared, and when they returned to bed he had ignored her warm body next to his in favour of the fitful sleep he had allowed to encapsulate him.

'You don't make any sense, woman.' The alarm was ringing violently close by, almost drowning out his voice with its edge of anger.

'I have to work,' Romance explained as her husband tried to pull her back into bed. He was still half-asleep and lacked the physical determination that showed in his voice.

'I thought you'd arranged time off for when I was here.'

'I sent you a note telling you Kingsley had died. It isn't my fault that you didn't come when you said you would.'

'I didn't know Kingsley would die,' Kunda retorted, 'and I didn't know ...'

Romance had pressed the 'off' switch on the clock and gone for a shower, leaving her husband's sentence half-finished behind her.

When she came back, Kunda still held an angry expression across his face. As she towelled a final sheen of water off her body, she could see him watching her, and his involuntary movement under the sheet. She sat on the bed beside him, and he pushed his hand high between her thighs.

'You'll have to be quick. I have to unlock,' she told him, not seeking pleasure for herself, but not wanting to leave him lustful and annoyed.

She lay smothered, with him on top of her pumping rhythmically. As soon as he had finished she kissed his stubbled cheek softly and pushed him away, to return to the shower.

Stephen phoned from Maputo, a few moments after she had unlocked the office and passed the gate keys to one of the men waiting to open the yard. She thought her boss was checking up on her, but he insisted that was not so. Then, to prove it, he read a long list of things he had forgotten to tell her before he had boarded the flight to the Mozambique capital. Her work list had almost doubled by the time she replaced the receiver.

At lunch, she returned upstairs to find Kunda dressed in a vest and boxers, drinking a Mosi from the stock she had left for him in the fridge, although she was surprised he had flipped the top on one so early. In the ashtray, there were three stubbed-out cigarette ends.

'I thought you might have come down and said hello when you got up,' she said, 'rather than sitting up here smoking and drinking beer.'

'I'm on holiday, woman. You shouldn't look so disapprovingly at your husband.'

Romance wanted his stay to be nice, for their time together to be special. It was silly to spoil things, she rationalized, when she was as much to blame for not being able to spend the time with her husband that he deserved.

'I'm sorry Kunda, but I have so much work to do, I must be in the office this afternoon. But tonight, we will go out and enjoy ourselves. We spend so little time together. We have a right to spoil ourselves occasionally.'

She quickly prepared sadza and relish for lunch, and before going back down took another beer from the fridge, opened the cap, and put it in front of her husband to show she was not really annoyed with him.

Romance took Kunda for a drink at a guest house off the main street, which catered mainly for visiting black South Africans and their families, and attracted many of the local black business owners to the terrace bar.

They ordered a second drink, mainly to break the awkward moments of silence that grew in length each time the conversation floundered. Romance tried to talk about her work, which irritated Kunda who, having drunk more beer during the afternoon while watching sport on the television, was prepared to vent his annoyance at being neglected. Young children running and chasing between the table inspired Romance to take her husband's hand and praise his patience with her not wanting to have children until they could afford to buy the house she so wanted.

'The extra money I'll be paid for running the new office will mean we will have enough money a lot sooner, and we will be together every day,' she told him, and gave his hand a squeeze to show the bliss she felt.

Kunda did not squeeze back, but turned to shout at one of the smaller children who collided with one of the empty chairs at their table, and then sobbed when his pursuers scrambled to avoid being reprimanded for their part in the mayhem.

Romance jumped to her feet to soothe the young warrior. Kunda rose at the same time, took his wife's arm, and led her from the bar without a word.

Later, in the middle of the night, Romance lay naked on the bed, foetal among damp, wrenched and crushed sheets. She felt satisfied, but in pain and hurting. This was not the usual way they enjoyed each other. Over her, her husband stood limp and outraged with jealousy.

'Is that the way it is now for you?' He did not wait for her answer. 'Drinking, food in restaurants, and the boss comes here for bompie.'

Romance squirmed to the edge of the bed, dropped her legs over the side, and made to stand.

'Is that what this place costs?' Again, Kunda did not wait for her to speak. He spoke and coughed as he pointed out the luxuries with his eyes. 'Bwana's small house. You.'

Her hand was within inches of his face, as his head fell back and his left forearm impeded the blow. His right thundered down, fist clenched, onto her temple, buckling her to the floor.

Later, he held her head in his lap and gently rocked her.

Romance tried to imagine what had caused her husband to address her in the way he had. She had tried to make his stay wonderful. After the bar, where the children seemed to irritate him, she had taken him to the True Zoo, and yes she could see he was not comfortable. Was it the fact that she was treated like a regular by the staff, the fact that there was no sadza on the menu, or that he had not brought out sufficient money to pay the bill? Whatever it was, she knew she did not deserve to be thought of in that way.

Kunda caressed her face with the back of his hand, knowing it was important to cajole his wife and obtain her forgiveness.

The yard teams thought she had a hangover. She let them continue with that belief.

They did not go anywhere for the remainder of his stay. The flat became an arena in which the competitors circled each other, occasionally coming together to test each others' reactions. Kunda was careful, not wishing to be rejected, sometimes offering over-elaborate flattery, and talking positively about their future housing, how well the car was performing both mechanically and in generating cash in its role as a taxi. Romance shopped for her husband's favourite food, ensured stocks of cigarettes and beer were sufficient, and spent as much time not in the office as her position would allow. In bed they had lain touching and caressing, and on the last night they made love without lust or passion, neither wanting to be accused of being the one who refused the other. Though, neither had asked. By the last day of his visit, a neighbour peering in through the window would have believed that trust between the couple had been restored.

'You have our savings for me to take back?' Kunda said, as he finished packing his bag.

'You are not going to put it in your bag, Kunda? What if you lose it?' Romance's tone was more than concerned.

'Don't worry. It's the best place. No one can steal it while we're going along, and when the bus stops I'll get out and make sure it isn't unloaded by mistake. Inside, if I fall asleep there are many hands.'

Before Kunda had arrived, it had been her intention to discuss with him her wish to travel to Jo'burg and help her sister. But now she didn't want to do anything that would cause more trouble between them. Her worries over Prudence would have to take second place to her marriage. She asked if Kunda had heard from his brother recently. Kunda could not understand why she was asking, and she did not want to tell him of Sonkwe's call on her.

'So where is your new hiding place?' Kunda enquired, impressed that he had not been able to find it during his hours alone in the flat.

Romance had not had reason to go to the safe since Mr Stephen had left, and it was only now that it occurred to her she did not have a key. Kingsley's key had been brought back, along with the files he had been intending to work on that last weekend. Everything was handed over to Mr Stephen. She had not thought to ask for it, and apart from her own money she could not think of any reason she would need it. Any cheques that arrived in the post she banked each day, and the yard staff were paid monthly in local currency directly into their bank accounts that Mr Robertson had insisted they all opened. She was the only person left who received salary, apart from Mr Stephen she presumed, paid in foreign currency. And she had been paid a little in advance before he left.

When she tried to explain, Kunda beat her with his belt, took her office keys and rifled through her desk, leaving with the petty cash and any banking monies.

The pain of the beating, the welts on her back and side, was not the worst of it, she deserved that for being so stupid she knew, nor was it the money she was responsible for that was now missing. She agonized, as all her hopes and aspirations drained away and she sat on the apartment floor, sobbing. Kunda's mouth had spewed vile words, describing a person she did not recognize, someone she never intended to become. He promised he would find himself a second wife, one he could trust.

CHAPTER ELEVEN

Stephen Simons sat in a police interview room at Harare airport, having been picked out from a line of passengers waiting to check in for his connecting flight.

A familiar setup: single table, two chairs, one either side. One policeman sat, another two stood. A fourth person, wearing cheap casual clothes, agitated to the side of where Stephen was sitting. This man was angry. He persistently poked his finger in Stephen's direction when he spoke. Stephen observed the dirt under the man's fingernails, and then checked the time on his watch. If he was not going to miss the connecting flight he realized he needed to get this matter sorted out, to get a move on. But he was damned if he was going to roll over. He had said his piece, and as the room finally went silent he looked at the officer sitting opposite and waited for him to speak.

Nobody spoke. The four black faces looked at him and waited.

'I've told you what happened; nothing has changed,' Stephen said without emotion, relaxed, but with an air of defiance.

The man standing next to him began shouting and hopping around. This time he was speaking in Shona, and the other policemen in the room joined in the conversation. Stephen had no clue as to what was being said, but it seemed the taxi driver was not getting it all his own way.

'Mr Simons, you must pay the taxi man the fare,' the policeman sitting opposite finally adjudged.

'I have paid,' Stephen responded.

'He says you have only paid half, and that you must pay the rest.'

Stephen explained once more: 'Two hours ago I took a taxi from here to the Monomotapa Hotel in the city centre. An hour ago I took this man's taxi back here from the same spot, and he's trying to charge double. I paid him the correct amount. He's trying to rob me. I will not give him the extra money.'

The officer again spoke in Shona, the taxi driver shouted back. This time, although Stephen did not know what was being said, he had the impression the taxi driver was accusing the officer of siding with a white tourist.

Stephen butted in: 'Excuse me sir, but you know what the correct fare from the city is, and I am in the right here. Taxi drivers ripping off tourists does not do your country any good. It gives you a bad name.'

There was another exchange in Shona, more heated on both sides this time. Stephen again looked at his watch.

'If you do not pay him the money, he is insisting that you are arrested.'

'Well I'm not giving him any more money and I am going to leave now to catch my plane.' Stephen stood and took out his wallet. Removing sufficient greenbacks to cover the disputed amount, Stephen offered to the policeman. 'I think you are an honest man, and I believe this man here is a thief. If you think the fare he is asking for is right, please give him the money. If you think he's been paid the right fare, you and your colleagues keep the money. Whatever you decide to do, I'll be happy with. And now I must catch my flight.' Stephen turned and left, closing the door firmly behind him.

oOo

Stephen took the in-flight magazine from the net on the rear of the seat in front of him and pressed the button on the arm to ease himself upright. On the front cover, a policeman was directing traffic in the city centre. Stephen smiled and took a bet with himself: the greenbacks he had left behind would have seen a three-way split, and one of those three would not have been the taxi driver. The seat next to him was, as were many others, empty. The aircraft taxied, stopped, waited and then accelerated down the runway before lifting over the city. He was glad of the soft drink when service began. Lowering the blind to exclude the sun, he continued to casually flick through the glossy well-thumbed pages.

A young woman, a few seats ahead, stood to retrieve something from her bag in the overhead locker. She was not tall: Stephen noticed her gain a few inches as she stretched, guessing she had gone on tiptoe. He looked at her neat figure. She reminded him of Chipo. The woman must have sensed someone staring in that instinctive way people have when they become the target of another person's attention. She twisted her head and met Stephen's stare. He averted his look back to the page he was not really reading. She did not have Chipo's eyes. A sadness, emanating deep in his abdomen, welled up inside his body, draining any smile from his face and filling his eyes. On the page in front of him was a picture of a large crane with a huge hook, lifting a motor launch from a marina. He remembered the large hook he had seen in the ceiling of Kingsley's workshop, and then tried to fight away the image of Chipo's perfectly formed body hanging there. Lifeless. Pointless. Dead.

'Is everything alright, sir?' the hostess enquired,

interrupting her journey along the aisle to undertake some errand further down the plane.

'Yes.' Stephen swallowed the remorse back and blinked to clear his vision.

'Can I get you anything?'

'No, really, I'm fine thank you.'

The plane banked over the mountains and entered Mozambique airspace.

It had not made any kind of sense to him. He had drawn the money for firewood and the hire of a truck from petty cash, according to the union agreement, and given it to Sanjay Johal when he had come to the office to inform him of the terrible news, and to return the safe key and other items Kingsley had been working on at home. He should have asked someone, probably Romance, how long the requirement remained in place for an employer to take financial responsibility for the funeral affairs of deceased employees' families. Not that it mattered: he would have happily, if happily could ever be the right word, paid it out of his own pocket.

Sanjay had arrived at the office at the end of the day with the goods he was returning, and an unmistakably heavy heart. The news of the second death had taken Stephen's feet from under him. Dropping his weight into the chair, he sat silently behind his desk for what seemed to be a period of time that did not exist; then he opened his drawer and set out two large whisky glasses. He poured himself a second, without taking notice of finishing the first, and pushed the bottle across the desk towards Sanjay, who had taken up the chair opposite him.

'Why?' Stephen guessed he was directing the question to the man in the expensive suit, a resigned look on his face and a wet coating of single malt on his lips. But in tone, it could just as easily have been a petition to God, a god, any god. The devil.

Sanjay shrugged his shoulders. 'It happens.'

'But why? I understand love, sort of. But life goes on. She still had a lot to live for.' Stephen seemed to be searching his brain as he spoke. A deep furrow creased his brow. 'Christ, she was beautiful.'

'I think that might have added to the problem. His relatives would have been queuing up.'

'To marry her?'

'For the cleansing. But I think any man would have considered her an admirable wife. She was devoted to Kingsley.'

Sanjay sipped his drink.

Stephen did not understand the cleansing reference, and his quizzical look deepened his frown.

'You don't think so?'

'No, I'm sure they were. It was the cleaning bit I didn't understand.'

'Cleansing … I assumed, following your own experience, you understood the background.'

'How does what I went through relate to Chipo killing herself?' Stephen was now more confused than ever.

'I'm sorry, I thought you knew. When a husband dies, there' is a ritual that the widow must go through, known as cleansing.'

'And?'

Sanjay shrugged, finished the remainder of the liquid in his glass, and answered as he began to leave.

'I guess it was something that neither woman could face, and each dealt with it in her own way. The lady involved in your debacle fled. When the headman's enforcers caught up with her, she refused to return. Things got out of hand and she ended up getting hacked to death.'

The pilot's voice interrupted his thoughts, the lights for 'seat belts' and 'no smoking' came on and the plane commenced descent over Beira. He had arranged for two meetings, before catching another flight up to the capital, Maputo. The plane's wheels sent spray high as they touched down, and a wave of hot, damp air greeted him as he descended the steps onto the runway. Hotter and more humid than Harare. A taxi driver opened the boot and Stephen lifted his bag in, the man making no effort to help. Stephen tried English, but earned a shrug. Knowing many of the streets were unnamed, and others were identified by various titles, which added to the resulting confusion, he held up a copy of the hotel brochure Romance had tucked into the envelope with his ticket and booking forms. Sinking back into the well-worn sprung seat Stephen wound down the window to relieve the distinct smell of perspiration and stale fried food. The drive, which Stephen had no way of telling was taking him in the most direct route to his hotel, skirted the port, which seemed to have an excess of shipwrecks close by. The new, tall buildings were no different from any other city, but the ornate colonial-style facades were an unexpected fascination, unkempt, with patchy peeling paint, allowing him to conjure up images of a bygone regime.

Suddenly realizing he had been in the cab far longer than he had anticipated, he tried to judge where he might be, but each turn seemed to lead from one praca into an identical one: each square with its palm trees, kids and young men in shorts and vests. Stephen leaned forward and tapped the driver on the shoulder with the brochure and pointed to the name. The driver pointed directly ahead to a large blue and white building, the Hotel Mozambique. It appeared this was the city centre.

With nothing pre-arranged for most of this first day, Stephen set aside his work to simply enjoy being the tourist in a country from which he had collected stamps as a youngster; he was now in a position to enjoy a childhood dream.

It was more the idea of the place that had captured his imagination, the magic of the name, than any researched knowledge. He had never read any books about it, although he had read articles in papers and magazines whenever his eye alighted on them. He realized he had never purchased a guidebook for the place and still did not possess one. But features in glossies, and stands he had seen at tourist expos, showed high-end lodges beginning to establish themselves.

Leaving the hotel, with most of his valuables deposited securely at reception, he walked in the opposite direction of a sign pointing to the railway station; he had come to believe railway stations were usually located in the drabber, more ghettoized part of a city. A few hundred yards on he could smell the salt breeze coming in off the sea. He turned onto Rua Correia Brito and then Avenida Kahora Bassa, and caught sight of a large church, grey with neglect. The old grandeur of the building suggested it was probably on the tourist map, but he decided not to bother unless on the way back it had started to rain.

On the seafront he could see a tall red and white concrete lighthouse, and turned in that direction. One day, with war a generation or two back, he could visualize five-star hotels and casinos fighting over beachfront. A huge carcass, a beached whale of a vessel, suddenly dominated his attention. He couldn't bring to mind anywhere he had visited that offered up so much distressed shipping.

Hot, he collapsed outside a cafe and ordered a cold drink. Two backpackers, who he placed as French Canadians, pointed him in the direction of Brave Heart market.

'It's signposted Tchunga Mayo. They've got everything, man, the whole place is fake.'

Stephen thanked them for their advice and used his shirt-sleeve to wipe away the sweat that the cold liquid seemed to immediately expel from his body, the moment he finished his first swallow.

He arrived back at the hotel without intention, but ready for a cold shower and a siesta, realizing he had not ventured inside the cathedral and had obviously taken a wrong turning on his halfhearted quest for the market.

He ordered 'jantar', an amazing platter of fruits de mer, at the Clube Nautico on Macuti beach with a prospective agent and stayed on to drink a second bottle of Vinho Verde to accompany his enjoyment of the sunset views over the Indian Ocean. The day after he was entertained by another hopeful, who drove him south along the coast for another heaped plate of prawns, clams, mussels, crayfish and several glasses of chilled Portuguese red. Being driven back, he wished now he had booked a rental car out of Beira to spend time driving along the coast south to Maputo the following day, although that would have meant delaying the meetings planned in the capital. Picking up the vehicle in the city and getting stuck simply driving it around the streets seemed crazy. The opportunities to spend a few days motoring, drinking cold beer and swimming in the clear ocean on these deserted white beaches seemed a crime to miss.

Landing that evening in Maputo after the short flight from Beira, he decided to cancel the return hop and arrange a car on a one-way rental.

Overfed and confident he could settle on one of the contacts he had made, Stephen set off with a newly purchased bodyboard. An hour out of the city, the sky darkened and a thunderstorm brought a deluge of rain. Heading north, the roads were worse than he had imagined and already he was aware that if he was going idle away some time sitting on beaches, punctuated by the odd plunge into the cooling waters of the Indian Ocean, his impromptu two-night trip was going to take a little longer. He drove across the Limpopo, and then out to Praia do Xai Xai. Having walked barefoot over the dunes onto the virtually deserted beach, he sat for an hour under a green plastic cape he had purchased from a roadside stallholder, looking out across the ocean waiting for the rain to stop. It didn't.

At Quissico, he checked the spare tyre was hard and the

jack was in place: a precaution he believed worthwhile, as the quantity of potholes and unmade road led him to understand both items would probably see use before his trip was over. He tried to remember whether tyre damage was a loss of deposit infringement, but could not be bothered to pull the agreement out of the glove compartment to scrutinize the small print, which he realized would probably in any case be in Portuguese.

The rain stopped, but the situation did not look as though it would last. He almost made it to the beach, but the smell of food alerted him to his hunger pangs and a lunchtime expedition won out.

'Ovos, faz favour.'

A stall in the market, which the dry spell had reinvigorated, seemed to be offering fried-egg or fish sandwiches. He signalled two with his fingers and ate one resting against the boot of his car, setting the other on the passenger seat to eat later on the beach. His chosen parking place, tight to a cement wall in the shade of a huge blue flowering jacaranda tree, had protected him at first. Before he was less than half way through his snack, a skinny kid with one leg missing below the knee, supporting himself on a roughly made wooden crutch, held out a mud-stained, begging hand. Stephen placed an uncounted amount of coins from his pocket into the small extended palm, and as if by magic or unseen two-way radio Stephen found himself surrounded by a chorus of small cupped hands, mouths speaking words he did not understand, but their demands were clear. The first child had been the recipient of all the coins in his pocket, and he knew a few notes given to those at the front would not be shared with those equally deserving at the back. He realized, after the event, his action was stupid, resulting in a ferocious scrabble as the children, many disabled, fought to seize the four screwed-up notes he had thrown into the middle of the group.

A woman wearing a blue head-scarf, sitting at the side of

a pile of firewood she was hoping to sell, looked at him with contempt as he drove slowly round her, angry she was not prepared to get out of his way. The chilling warning of staying to well-trodden paths in case of uncleared mines was ever-present as he realized she too was missing limbs – both her legs, from above the knee.

Stephen had rehearsed the phrase from a thin gratis guidebook which came with the car, when he pulled over and stuck his head out of the window.

'Faz favour. Tem marginal?'

The road signs were minimal and he had little in the way of the local language to understand the reply he was given. He shrugged his shoulders and pointed.

'Praia?'

The man he had pulled alongside smiled.

'You want beach?'

'Please.' Stephen smiled and sighed in his relief.

The man pointed him straight on and then off to the right.

'Very beautiful. The lagoons.' Then looked up at the sky and shrugged.

'Obrigado,' Stephen thanked him.

The man in the brown suit had been right, but rather than sheltering under his cape on this occasion Stephen found a strategic point to park and remained in the car contemplating the trials of life in a country so beautiful, even in the rain. He took the last mouthful of his now cold egg sandwich and headed north to the beach at Zavora.

The rain coming in on the wind off the sea, and the realization that the beach was at the end of a track ten miles off the main road, brought about a change of mind. Stephen traced his route on the map and decided to head for Barra, cutting off the main road at Lindela, in the direction of Inhambane, hoping not to miss the sand track, before Tofu, to the beach.

The rain stopped an hour after sunset. He ate dinner

alone and spent the evening talking to an English couple, at The Great Barra Reef Resort.

Waking late to the sound of parrots arguing in the mangroves, his inclination to swim was driven away by the sight of swelling rain clouds congregating above the shoreline. Instead he offered a backpacker a ride north. But she bailed when she became conscious that his route to rejoin the main road would take them too far south. She opted for a short trip on a motorboat for thirty cents. Stephen dropped her at the port and went on his way.

Ignoring the nearby town of Maxixe, except for topping up the tank and buying water, Stephen made it easily to the main road and started on a leisurely foray northward, only slightly frustrated at the lack of swim-time. There's always another beach to find.

oOo

Sitting in bed, enjoying the view over the sea, the sheet pushed down to his waist, Stephen smiled inwardly despite feeling more than a little guilty. The light smell of salt and seaweed were in the air, carried on a breeze that did little more than caress. Lounging over drinks on the terrace the previous evening, the sound of Simon and Garfunkel reminded him of Romance, as it always did, and of course the office. She was there holding the fort alone for the first time. Over a crackly line, switched through to the flat in the evenings since the attempted robbery, he spoke to Romance and was reassured that all was well and that his extended stay should not concern him. Although after replacing the receiver he did feel she sounded a little low. The sheet moved slightly, exposing his leg. Gently he eased it back without disturbing the body next to him.

He had recognized her sitting on a wall a short distance from where he had bought petrol.

'Not good for lifts today?' he had asked, pulling

alongside and sticking his head out of the window. Cracking a smile in a suntanned face gained from spending two months lazing in Camps Bay just outside Cape Town, his fleeting backpacker acquaintance threw her stuff onto the back seat and gladly re-established her lift.

She was South African, but now lived with her parents in New Zealand. The journey was a gap year, revisiting childhood memories. They had moved away when she was nine. After Beira, she intended to travel overland to Harare, then out of Zim at Kariba, hoping to pick up a lift down to Vic Falls. After that, through Bots and back to Jo'burg to catch her flight home.

'Don't you worry about being picked up by bad people?' Stephen had asked, concerned for a female travelling alone.

'What, like you,' she had teased.

'I'm ok,' he had assured her.

'I was travelling with a guy from back home. But he turned out to be a real arsehole. He caused trouble when there wasn't any. I dumped him before I left Camp's. I've had a great time since then.'

At the turn-off to Vilankulo, Stephen's passenger indicated she was intending to spend some time on the islands but was happy to spend the night on the mainland if he wanted.

Stephen checked them into a beachfront thatched cottage with a double and single. He graciously declined the first shower and found his chalet mate clearly occupying one side of the double bed, wrapped in a short towel, when he emerged in boxers, T-shirt and flip-flops.

True, the thought of sex had more than crossed his mind but he had reckoned on dinner and a bottle of wine before he broached the possibility. And then there was his unprepared state, not having equipped himself with condoms before leaving. As it turned out, his concerns proved unnecessary. His guest had an outer pocket of her bag stuffed with them; obviously, he realized, she was not looking to rely solely on her thumb to ensure the success of her passage.

The reflection in the mirror of his white freckled torso contrasted against the deeply tanned, half-covered naked girl in his bed. Cut in half, top to bottom, by a crumpled, sweat-damp sheet, the image burned his eyes. It wasn't just the view: there was a sound outside, not right there, further off in the middle distance, that he could not place, but reminded him and added to the stimuli. The shadow darkening his nose and upper lip probably tipped the balance.

He was not a tall lad at fourteen. He had sprung up, everyone said, like a beanstalk at the point when he was convinced his growing years were coming to an end. He still could not, sixteen years later, settle on whether his actions had been driven by the urge to protect, or by jealousy. Had he used the string side of the violin, the damage he caused would surely have been worse. Blood splattered out, and the much-prized musical instrument broke in two at the neck from the force of the blow, the strings giving up their last performance. He angrily threw the weapon to the floor, and ran in tears from the bedroom to a hiding place from years earlier, behind the garden shed. Sobbing, he pressed his cheeks against the old moss-coated stone wall until they shared the same temperature.

Stephen's father managed the local office of an obscure building society which he had taken over ten years earlier, after leaving a well-paid position at one of the high profile 'big five' banks when the pressure to sell product in preference to providing banking services became too much. His mother, quite the opposite of his father, both visually and in temperament, and who his father referred to with a tone of endearment as his *Little Fox*, headed up the fund-raising department of an international charity. Neither got home until after dark, and Stephen did not emerge until both were back. The large Victorian semi had been searched from attic to basement, and the shed had been investigated on two occasions.

It did not all come out at once. The event was reported to his parents by a teacher at Helen's school, who had overheard pupil gossip and had matched it to a dreadful change in behaviour from a normally well-respected student.

'This is probably none of my business, but insomuch as it is, I believe …'

Stephen's parents, having both given up a half-day at the office to answer the summons, sat across the over-stacked desk from a teacher they had previous met rarely on the occasional parent-teacher evenings. They had waited in silence to hear of the terrible deed that they could not or would not place in their imagination.

The teacher continued, picking her way through the anticipation cautiously: '… the cause of your daughter's recent change in her approach to things'.

'So what is it you think our daughter has been up to?' Jane asked, more than slightly irritated with what she saw as the pussy-footing attitude of the woman sitting across from her, who did not look a great deal older than her charge. But doing the maths, she guessed five years plus was the number.

'Your son … Stephen, is it?' She waited for affirmation before continuing, but was interrupted.

Derek shuffled forward onto the edge of his seat.

'Our son doesn't even go to school here.' He was preparing to leave, unwilling to have anything detrimental levied at his boy.

'As I said when you first came in, it is only with the impact his actions have had on Helen that I felt the matter should be aired.'

'Well, what is it that you think Stephen has done to cause such trauma, which frankly I can't say I've noticed at home, have you Derek?'

'Helen is Helen, she's always been temperamental, but I understand that it is normal for all teenage girls to have attitude lurking under the surface.' Derek spoke as if he had given the question some substantial prior consideration, but without realizing he had become fixated with a dark mark that had begun to appear from under the shoulder strap of the teacher's dress as she moved her arm.

'Apparently he assaulted Helen's boyfriend, hitting him in the face with her violin.'

'Helen does not have a boyfriend. She goes around with a group at weekends, when she isn't practising, but I would know if there was someone special. And as for the violin, that was stolen from under her seat on the bus. She's borrowing one from her music teacher as he's away on holiday for a couple of weeks. We've said that we'll find the time next weekend to purchase her a replacement.'

'I haven't made myself clear. I understand that her boyfriend and her music teacher are one and the same.'

'That's bloody ridiculous.' Jane, exasperated, stood to signify the meeting was over.

'Have you met Stephen?' Derek asked.

'No, but ...'

'Well, if you had you would know just how ridiculous what you are saying is,' Derek butted in, standing to accompany his wife in her imminent departure.

The teacher rose to gain equal stature.

'Mr and Mrs Simons. Please sit down. This is not something I have made up. Over the past few days, it has become the main topic of gossip in the yard. Please sit. I don't want this incident to get out of hand.'

Jane wavered.

'How is it this nonsense got round the place?'

'I assume Helen told a friend and that friend told another and before you know it... Well, you can imagine,' the teacher suggested.

Seeing the hesitation, Derek quietly returned to his seat.

'Why would Stephen do such a thing? He's devoted to his sister,' he asked, trying to bring some reason to what had been suggested.

'Apparently, the story circulating is that he found Helen in bed with Christopher, I believe that's his name, and in a fit of anger took a swing at him with Helen's violin. Apparently it was completely destroyed.'

'What, we are sitting here discussing Helen being upset, and Stephen ruining her violin, and it's only now you see fit to mention that I've been paying her music tutor to shag her in my own home.' Jane's face had turned purple.

'Most girls of her age are probably having some form of sexual experience, Mrs Simons, and I'm sure her music was not suffering. Her performance in the orchestra had been outstanding until this matter arose. However, I am worried about Helen becoming the centre of the school's amusement, which I have seen before can quickly turn to bullying and intimidation. And, I think you should also be concerned at what is in your son's head. It may be some form of counselling or anger management is appropriate.'

Outside, and back in the car, Jane expressed her dissatisfaction with the state education system.

'Did you see, I swear she had a bloody tattoo on her shoulder.'

Against their father's wishes, but on their mother's insistence, Stephen and Helen were packed off to board at separate public schools, without waiting until the beginning of the following term – Helen's destination more prestigious than her brother's, and further away.

'I don't know what you're hoping to achieve,' Derek had argued.

'I'm not having my son marked down for the rest of his life as some retard with mental problems, and I'm certainly not having this house turned into a set from Lolita. If she wants to destroy her future, she can do it well away from here.'

Derek phoned Helen's music tutor and cancelled all further lessons, warning that if any action was taken against Stephen, Jane would take it upon herself to see he became unemployable.

At Helen's wedding in 1994, the incident had been a source of amusement between them all as an oblique reference was made during one of the speeches to indicate if ever the groom mistreated Helen, he could be certain there was one member of the family that would ensure he faced the music.

The episode in the teacher's office was relayed almost verbatim by his father, over drinks shortly after he had graduated, conceding that his mother may not have been wrong to send him and his sister off to public school.

'Knock Knock. Bom dia.' A voice at the open-fronted chalet retrieved Stephen from the fleeting snatches of his past. Stephen flicked the loose tail of the sheet over the partly exposed body before inviting in the waiter, who presented him with the tray of coffee he had ordered the night before.

The following days were spent driving along main roads, through narrow village streets and down onto beach tracks. Regardless of the laid surface, even where groundworks had been intended, the ride was very much the same; jerky, rough and, at speed, treacherous, in what seemed to be constant rain. And when it stopped, the threat of more from dark clouds blowing in off the ocean removed from Stephen's mind any thought of the traditional sun-drenched beach vacation. Everyone Stephen passed the time of day with insisted that by this time of the year, the rains should be over.

Instead, he meandered among the shacks and shelters erected on the beaches which by day were busy markets, trading in everything the local villagers could possibly need and many items he found difficult to visualize any would want. At night, stock was locked away, display surfaces were uncovered to reveal pool tables, makeshift bars filled up with beer cans of 3M and Laurenco, bottles of whisky and a lethal cassava home-brew. Music was pumped out of oversized beat-boxes. Stephen lost more games than he won, laughed a lot, danced a little and drank more of the local hooch than his legs could handle. He thought more visitors should venture from their five stars, but from the few Europeans he occasionally spotted, where he had ended up was clearly not on the tourist map.

Stephen returned the car to the hire centre a day early, leaving his dreams in the boot unused.

CHAPTER TWELVE

Romance's father had left shortly after her marriage, travelling north and over the border, with the intention of locating his younger brother who he had not been in contact with for many years. Age was creeping up, and he did not wish to pass from this world without feeling the warmth of the man he had brought up like his own son.

Talking to a person travelling south he had been led to believe Charles was in the north, but the man could not remember in which town, even for certain which country he had made the acquaintance. It had taken him three years from hearing the rumour to leaving. His simple plan was to move from town to town, living on her bride price.

'The man is a fraud,' she had told her father. 'He's only looking to bleed us dry of food and drink. Who spoke of your brother first?' she had asked.

'I did,' her father insisted.

'You meet a man in a bar, and he knows your long-lost brother. He's a fraud, I tell you.'

'When you're married I will have no one. So what difference will it make? My brother left to work in the north. Maybe he never met him. Maybe he's just a chi gebenga in Tonga. But it has given me the ambition to go and look, and there's nothing to say I won't find him anyway.'

Romance's mother had died ten years earlier, at the stillbirth of a much wanted brother for Romance. After her father's declared intention to travel north, it had taken three years for the marriage to happen, and then only finally when her father settled on a derisory amount of money and a cow, which he quickly sold. Kunda saved what he could, and Romance added to the meagre amount a paltry sum she had managed to secrete away. The total lobola accepted was small and her father's friends told him he was stupid to settle for so little for such a fine daughter. Kunda and Romance were in love, and if her father was ever to find his brother, and the couple were ever to marry, the deal had to be agreed. So it was.

No one mentioned Prudence disappearing. But everyone knew she had travelled south to be with Kunda's brother. Once she had gone, it was as though she had never existed in the village. The name Prudence never left her father's lips again and Romance knew better than to raise the name.

Now things were different, the relationship between the married couple had changed. Romance had nobody to speak on her behalf. Kunda was a stubborn man, and if they were to be happy together again, she needed someone to speak to a member of his family so they could persuade him to take back the words he had said and allow their life together to be everything they had planned. She had already forgiven the blows he had landed on her. She thought of writing to her sister, when Stephen returned, to arrange a visit, taking the money she had not been able to retrieve from the safe and give to Kunda. Her thoughts focused on persuading Prudence to beg Sonkwe to speak on her sister's behalf. But sadly she was not even sure Prudence was still of this world. She thought then of approaching her minister after the service, and asking him to write to a member of the church in her own village. But he could not be trusted, and she feared where placing such responsibility might lead.

Finally, she decided to make an appointment to see Mr Johal. He would know the right person, she felt sure. But she would wait until Stephen returned, so she could obtain her money. Solicitors were not cheap, and she would want to settle her bill there and then, not ask him to wait for payment.

Stephen returned to the office on the Monday, bright, his face looking healthily weathered, reflecting the brilliant sunshine he claimed he enjoyed on the only day he was away from the coast.

'You sounded as though all was under control here, so I took a diversion along the Zambezi Delta for a spot of game viewing.

'That must have been interesting for you.' Romance's curiosity was almost satisfied.

'Bit of a mistake really. A guide travelling on the plane back told me the game had been seriously depleted during the war, and that I was lucky I didn't decide to go into Gorongosa National Park. Apparently it was occupied by the Renamo freedom fighters, and thousands of land mines have been left there,' Stephen explained.

'Sounds very dangerous.'

'I'm not sure how true it was. He was from Zim, the Lower Zambezi part. I got the impression he was trying to put me off everything to do with other locations.'

'I have heard the Lower Zambezi is a good place for seeing animals,' Romance said, unsure of herself on a subject of which she knew little.

'Have you been there?'

'Animals scare me.'

'But you've seen the Big Five?'

'I've never even seen a lion.'

'You're joking, Romance. People travel, pay fortunes to travel halfway round the world to come on safari. It's wonderful having all this in your own country. On your doorstep,' Stephen enthused.

'Mr Stephen, I'm sure in England you do not live in a zoo, or have wild animals roaming through the streets. Most people just want to live in a civilized country and be able to build successful lives. If it wasn't for tourism, most of the game would have disappeared. That was the way it was in '81 when this country was one of the poorest in southern Africa.'

The telephone ringing broke the impending debate into which Romance felt she was in danger of being dragged. And when she had taken the call, the work was again underway. Two supervisors had come in to collect their worksheets and Stephen had retreated into his office.

At the end of the day, Romance heard Stephen on the phone to Sanjay Johal, while she was collecting some files from the solid stack that had accumulated on Kingsley's desk. Each night since Kunda had left, she had taken two or three files up to her apartment, as she now called it, and pored over them, trying to evaluate the work required and the methodology Kingsley had used.

At lunchtime she had asked Stephen for the key to the safe so that she could retrieve some of her money.

'Are you going to buy something nice?'

She told him it was not for a purchase, but she was intending to seek advice from Mr Johal and she would need to settle his bill. And redress both the plundered petty cash and the clients' cash payments Kunda had stolen. But these last points she did not mention.

'Are you in some sort of trouble, Romance?' he enquired, with genuine concern. 'Maybe I can be of assistance.'

Romance explained the falling out she had had with Kunda because she had not been able to give him the money she had saved.

'This is all my fault, Romance. I should have given you

the key before I left, regardless of the fact your money was in the safe. Did it cause any other problems?'

Romance explained that a few items normally delivered COD she could not settle, but none of the suppliers withheld the goods. All had been happy to collect on their next visit, when she gave grounds for the oversight.

'I will speak to Sanjay, and ask him to invoice me personally for his fee.'

Romance had protested, but Stephen had been insistent. In truth Romance had been quite nervous about how much it would cost. Solicitors, she knew, had a reputation for charging excessive fees. She had to admit to herself that it did lift some of the burden she felt over her decision.

Sanjay Johal was leaving for Maun, and would not be returning until Thursday, but had agreed to meet with Romance on the Friday morning.

oOo

'Romance, may I call you by your first name, I feel we are already friends.'

'Romance would be very acceptable, Mr Johal,' she said cautiously, not wishing to be viewed as a young woman who could be treated with insignificance.

'Romance, first let me apologize for not being able to see you sooner, but my trip to Bots was a longstanding arrangement. Now what is your problem, and how may I help. Nothing too serious, I hope.'

They were sitting in the bright offices of Cron Johal Solicitors at Law, situated on the top floor of one of the town's taller buildings.

Romance explained her situation in slightly embarrassed tones.

'I assume your marriage was a traditional ceremony. If that is the case there will have been no paperwork, simply the witnesses. And a wife, after divorce, I must advise you, will receive no part of the family estate. The car, your savings and anything else you may have of value would be the property of your husband. Whilst you would not of course be destitute, you have a reasonably good job and your employer obviously values you; it is not something I would generally recommend.'

'I'm not looking for a divorce, I'm sorry if I did not make myself clear. I love my husband, but he is a very stubborn man and he said things I'm sure he did not mean. I thought you might have a colleague in the area of my village that could approach him and speak on my behalf. If I had family in the village, I would get word to them to mediate with his family, but unfortunately I have no one I can call upon in this matter.'

'Whilst I do not like to turn business away, Romance, I feel that in this case, once solicitors become involved, it will not become easier to resolve. The law, and those who represent it, are both asses on occasion,' Sanjay smiled. 'Is there nobody at all who could approach your husband?'

'Nobody I would want to share my feelings with,' Romance replied, feeling somewhat at a loss.

'If that is the case, I would suggest that maybe you get a message to the headman of your village and ask him to speak with Kunda. Your husband will surely respect his intervention.'

Romance did not consider it an ideal solution, but agreed that the suggestion had merit and that it was a route she would explore. She thanked Sanjay and stood to leave.

'May I walk you back to your office? Whilst I was in Bots I met someone who might prove to be a useful contact for Stephen: I know he is keen to see the business develop new offices.'

Romance spent the weekend writing and rewriting the letter she had decided to send to the headman of her village. Whatever words she put on paper, she could not make them say what it was she wanted to convey. The headman, she knew, would not look favourably on her request. Men owned their wives, bought by the lobola, and he would agree that a husband could ignore his wife for as long as he chose. And then there was having the letter delivered. The newspaper was always reporting sacks of mail being found dumped in the bush. Even recorded delivery could not be relied upon. No, the headman was not the answer, she had decided by the time she pulled the bed sheets up high under her chin on Sunday night.

By the end of the following week, she had settled on the idea of writing to the owner of the lodge where Kunda was employed. She believed the owner was a good man and his wife ran a clinic, supported by charitable donations from lodge guests, for very young orphans whose parents had died of AIDS. Yes, they were good people, they would speak to Kunda and convince him to reconcile his differences with her, she felt certain.

CHAPTER THIRTEEN

Empty bottles were now smashed. The new accountant had set up a system that made life more difficult. Previously it had been easy to stash an empty after the morning stocktake, and substitute it for a half-used one the following night, particularly if the lodge was busy.

'Some guests don't have the manners to stop when it's free.' Kunda regularly explained away the high volume of liquor consumption.

Earlier, he had washed out a Lion bottle and replaced the beer with brandy. Kunda thought the new control system was stupid. And the idea of guests signing for their drinks had been strongly vetoed by the owner.

'It makes it seem that we don't trust them, plus it's irritating having to sign for everything,' the owner had told the accountant when the idea was suggested.

Kunda had seen the torchlight coming along the path towards him, as he finished clearing down the tables. He guessed it was the accountant snooping around after everyone else had gone to bed. Mr Jackson had installed himself in a bungalow just the other side of the lodge's security fence, but Kunda knew he held a key for one of the gates that was always locked and never normally used. Quickly, Kunda skimmed a dinner plate out across the surface of the river. Tonight it was flowing wide and smooth under a full white moon, which gave it the appearance of grey sheet metal. Kunda pointed to the ripples the plate had caused.

'I think there are bad people on the river tonight,' he said.

The two men didn't like each other and both knew it.

'Hippos,' Mr Jackson countered.

'Canoes. You should keep watch if you're going to be out late, Mr Jackson. Some of these robbers are very dangerous.'

'I think you're wrong, Kunda. The moon is too bright and there's very little cloud. Not a good night for skulduggery.' Mr Jackson shone his Maglite along the bank to show willing.

'Can I get you anything before I lock up, sir?' Kunda offered, knowing the very tall bean-stick of a man with thinning hair and a face that never smiled, enjoyed his drink.

Kunda's offer was not rejected. And interpreting a small one with a lot of water as a large one with little water was also the right decision.

Kunda returned with the glass of whiskey and waited next to Mr Jackson. After a few moments of embarrassed silence Mr Jackson left.

'Good night Kunda.' Mr Jackson said and headed off, nightcap in hand.

'Good night sir. And keep an eye out, there are snakes this time of year as well.'

When the light was at a safe distance, Kunda moved along the path after him and watched as Mr. Jackson unlocked the gate went through and locked it after him.

Sure that there was no one left lurking around, Kunda slipped quietly down to the jetty and unlashed the five canoes, giving them a gentle shove with his foot out into the river.

The deed done, Kunda sat in the security guard's hut, a small squalid and dilapidated wooden shed, sharing his perks. In flickering candlelight, KWV was poured into broken-handled china cups, with a few sandwiches that had been cobbled together in the kitchen; food that had been pre-ordered, then later turned away by the guests. Some of the women, especially the Americans, seemed to have no appetite: skinny and rude, and the older ones the rudest of all. To Kunda, on American satellite TV stations many seemed overfed and fat, but none of those seemed to visit his restaurant.

Kunda always looked to avoid a late shift, particularly at the weekend. But after the visit with his wife, and now not being flush with money, staying behind to serve the stragglers supported his eating and drinking habits without dipping into his own wallet. And, on several occasions, he had been able pilfer more valuable items he could sell in the township.

Most of the security guards had day jobs and slept, never leaving the hut from the start of the shift to the end. As long as Kunda looked after whoever was on duty from time to time, they were of little concern.

Between mouthfuls, Kunda told the guard about his late-night encounter with the accountant.

The last part, involving the canoes, he kept to himself.

'I'm going,' Kunda said, pouring a little more KWV into the guard's cup and wrapping the beer bottle, now more than half empty, in an old newspaper.

Kunda's car was parked the other side of the barrier and he did not want to be seen leaving with a bottle. Not that there was likely to be anyone about at this time of night, except maybe the accountant doubling back, waiting in the shadows in the hope of catching him out.

By the time Kunda reported in for work the following

day, a guide with a powerful outboard on the back of a RIB had located and towed back four of the canoes.

'The boss wants to see you,' the receptionist called to Kunda as he was passing through, heading in the direction of the dining area.

Kunda looked suspicious. Normally instructions concerning service came via a sheet pinned up in the kitchen. He hesitated.

'He's in the office. I don't think he's very happy,' the receptionist added before returning to what he had been doing.

Kunda had a habit of slouching and dragging his feet when he was in trouble. When he was being reprimanded, he took to gazing upwards from a head slightly bowed. Consciously or unconsciously he began to take up this demeanour. Had Mr Jackson seen him leaving the security guard's hut? Had he caught the security guard asleep and drunk? Had the security guard blamed him for providing the liquor?

Kunda stood on the polished ochre-coloured cement path outside the boss's office and waited, shining his shoes on the back of his trouser legs as he did. A gecko ran up the wall and began picking off small insects from the underside of the stick roof. Kunda watched it for a moment, but his mind was elsewhere. Why had he been summoned? The variety of possible offences presented themselves.

The office door was ajar: he could have 'Knock-Knocked', but did not want to accelerate the process he was facing. Inside, he could see the boss of the security company seated and the guard Kunda had been drinking with, standing, cap on, shoulders down. Kunda could not hear what was being discussed. Seated behind the desk, Craig Graves, owner of Zimwani lodge, was speaking. Without warning, the security boss jumped up and Kunda saw the huge black hand slap the guard hard round the side of the head, sending his cap spinning, and knocking him to his knees.

'Fokken doff.'

Craig Graves stood, and leaned with both hands on his desk.

'That's enough.'

At the same time, having leaned forward, he saw Kunda making ready to slip away quietly.

'Kunda. Come in, please.'

He had missed his chance. Kunda thought of making an excuse, but realized that any lame pretext would not adequately override whatever it was that was being discussed.

Stepping in through the doorway, he took a sideways glance at the guard, who had now got to his feet. His uniform looked as if he had slept in it, and his eyes were red-raw, which Kunda put down to a large intake of dagga.

'Kunda, are you not well? You look down.'

'I'm well, sir.'

'I understand you saw people on the river last night?' Mr Graves enquired, sitting back down in his chair.

'No. There was ripples on the water, close to the bank, but I didn't see anyone, sir.'

'Why didn't you alert the guard?'

'Mr Jackson was out sir, so I warned him. I thought he would do something if he thought it was thieves, sir.' Kunda had lifted his head slightly, less diffident.

'Thank you, Kunda, that will be all.'

Kunda took his time walking out, in the hope of capturing the conversation between Craig Graves and the security boss. Snippets of the louder elements were audible as he hovered outside.

'Paying you, Mr Ndebele, for security guards that sleep on duty, is not acceptable. Mr Jackson will be deducting a substantial amount from this month's invoice,' Mr Graves asserted.

Mr Ndebele protested that it was only an isolated

incident and that only payment for one night should be withheld. He argued that the guard caught asleep had worked during the day as a policeman, that he had a sick wife and many children to support.

'I'm more than tempted to bring security in-house. If we have any more problems, that's what will happen. And I would strongly suggest you install clocking points around the perimeter so you can be sure your men are doing the rounds.'

'Mr Graves, they are expensive, they cost a lot of money, I would need to have them imported from down south. And you want to stop a lot of money from my invoice. How am I meant to buy equipment, get new uniforms and pay my staff?' Mr Ndebele protested.

Mr Graves rose, stretched his hand across the desk.

'I'm sure you would will find a way.'

Mr Ndebele shook the hand offered.

'You are a very determined man, Mr Graves. You are making life very hard for me.'

Ndebele pushed the guard towards the door, swinging his hand in the direction of the previously slapped ear. The guard rolled with it, ducking to pick up his cap at the same time.

Kunda did not see the point of being called to the office. The only person he had told his lie to was Mr Jackson, so the boss must have known of the conversation. Whatever the case, he felt he was not in trouble, but would keep his head down for a while.

Three nights later, one of the cottages was looted. The open structure was situated so close to the riverbank that during the rainy season it flooded, and regularly experienced crocs just below deck level. While the guests had been on a night drive their bags were ransacked, and their cameras stolen.

The alleged culprits were tracked the following day by Mr Ndebele and one of his detectives. The accused, two fishermen from a small village five miles upriver, were taken to the police station, beaten and charged, only to be released when their relatives paid a large greenback bribe. The cameras were never recovered.

o0o

'Hey, Bulongo.' Isaac slapped the top of Kunda's car as it pulled up at the nearby stop sign. 'You want to go graze?'

With a little more money in his pocket now, Kunda had stopped working the late shift. He leaned over and pushed the passenger door open. The car behind blared its horn. When Kunda continued to wait for Isaac to get in, the driver eased forward and lightly shunted Kunda's back bumper.

Kunda threw open his door and jumped out, narrowly missing a bakkie turning the corner. The driver of the rusted 4x4 behind, and his three passengers, jumped out and grabbed Kunda in a tumbling maul.

The group stopped laughing to shout rude remarks at other road users who were complaining at the inconvenience being posed.

'Long time no see, Bulongo.'

Vehicles backed up along the road and round the corner quickly, and with the signs of serious disorder beginning to bear down on the group, Kunda jumped back in next to Isaac and drove off.

'Who were they?'

'Some guys I know from Lusaka.'

'How did they know it was you?'

'They didn't till I jumped out.'

Isaac thought they looked like trouble, but didn't ask Kunda what they were doing here. He was of the opinion there were some things it was better not to know.

Kunda paid for their fried chicken and fries, and told Isaac that he could buy the Mosis at the beer hall later.

Kunda had not shown his face there since he returned from visiting Romance, either choosing to work late or attempting to word up Jabu. With little cash he had decided she was his best bet, but since her husband had returned, he had only managed to meet with her once, and then only for half an hour. Tonight he had decided to see if the young chicken was about, fuck the cost. All the talk in the world would make no difference, she wanted money for it, he knew that. There were plenty of other women around, but they all knew him. And that was not in his favour.

Kunda regretted his outburst with Romance. She had been a good source of money, and now he was not sure if he could still rely on her. She was his wife and he was more than capable of forcing her to do whatever he demanded, nobody would argue against that, but he would have to drag her back to live in the village. This was not something he craved. There would be fights and she would not earn the greenback she was being paid. He decided he would leave it, let some weeks pass, and if she didn't find a way of getting the rest of the money to him he would write to her, tell her he missed her, and that he would pay a visit the next time he could get extra days off.

Kunda bought a half-jack from the general store and sipped from it, the cheap liquor cutting his throat and unwinding his head. He sat, waiting, in the shade cast by the wall of the beer hall. It didn't take the scarred little chicken long to find the potential income loitering on her patch and Kunda, biddable from drinking the spirit, was easy prey to her inflated demands.

'Bulonga, you no need to go to the beer hall, you stay with me. We do it some more,' she had purred over him each time he had shown signs of leaving. 'I have plenty Mosi, you want spirit, I run out get whatever it is you want.'

A trip for spirit, and another for food, reduced the money in his wallet each time by considerably more than the value of the goods purchased.

The following morning Kunda fell into his car, with five dollars US in his wallet. He was working lunchtime and needed to get a couple of hours' sleep. The road was quiet, it was a lot earlier than he had realized. He was not focusing well. Racing the engine, grinding the gears, he swung the car out from the parking area. Burning rubber, windows down and music loud, he mixed himself a high-speed cure.

Redlining the speedometer he overtook several trucks, travelling five miles mostly on the wrong side of the road, throwing dust into sandy clouds each time he clipped the dry unmade verge. He hardly saw the bakkie until it was running alongside him and blocking his way back in. He blasted the horn a few times, before recognizing the vehicle and the four guys from Lusaka.

'Hey, Bulongo, we didn't see you last night,' the driver shouted across as they vied for position. 'What the hurry, your wife after you?'

The bakkie edged forward, sufficient to mushroom a cloud of grit and dust in on Kunda, thick enough to block the image of the truck closing in on him. The horn sounded like a train, Kunda knew it was somewhere, he checked his mirrors. Then, with the front grille blocking out everything across his windscreen, the dust cleared and Kunda wrenched the steering wheel, spinning the car off into a barren field as the chrome-faced beast thundered on by.

'Fuck, that was close.' The four guys had pulled him clear. One of them handed him a piece of rag, which he used to stem the blood pouring from his nose. Another rolled a long thick joint, twisted the end, and lit it. Had it not been for the necessity of sitting still with his head tilted back, Kunda's mad rage would have known few bounds.

'You nearly fucking killed me!'

The manufacturer of the joint, the smallest of the group, with an oversized round face and a complexion not dissimilar from the texture of the field they were occupying, passed Kunda the joint.

'You need to be more warried, man.'

Kunda missed lunch, sending a message to the lodge saying he had a fever. To add credibility to the fever story, he also took another three days off.

'Kunda, are you feeling better?' It was one of the guests for whom he had served dinner on their first night, the last time he had been at work.

'Yes madam, I was lucky: it was just a mild touch of malaria,' he told the woman, who he believed was Dutch, adding warmly, 'I hope you have a good journey home, and that we will see you back here soon.'

Her butler arrived with two soft travel bags. She thanked him with a ten-dollar bill from her purse.

'I'll put these in the Land Rover. Please have a nice trip,' the butler said, slipping the note into his pocket and taking the bags out to the car park.

'You make sure you have medicine at home. If your children got sick it could be very serious.' She passed him a note, which he did not examine before tucking it into his waistcoat.

'Thank you, madam. I always make sure my children are well cared for, but sometimes it is difficult.' Kunda did not know why she thought he had children, maybe she thought everyone had children. It was not something he felt inclined to redress.

Lunch was normally quiet; most guests were out, picnicking on one of the small islands, game viewing or buying souvenirs in the village. Only arrivals would normally take lunch on-site. Kunda checked the sheet in the kitchen. Just two, not expected until two-thirty. There were two waiters, clearing the last of the breakfast buffet dishes away. He told them to make sure the cruets and mustards were full, that the plates and cutlery were clean and back from the wash-up, then he assigned himself the job of collecting clean linen from the laundry.

'Where's Jabu?' Kunda had walked around the side of

the workshop, along the rough path perimeter of the vegetable garden and on to the laundry block, which was tucked away from guests' view and the smells of the kitchen. He could have walked along the cinder path from the car park, but did not want to be seen doing a menial task, carrying a large bundle of dirty tablecloths.

'You should stay away, if Jabu's man see you …,' the fat old woman who checked the stuff in and out told him, not finishing her sentence with words, just pulling a face as if a bad smell were under her nose, and shaking her head.

Kunda dumped the dirty stuff on the floor, not waiting for the woman to count the items. He picked up the stack of neatly pressed and folded dining-room linen from the table and left without responding.

'Psst. Psst.'

Lines of brilliant white sheets flapping in short gusts of air blocked the line of sight to the psst'er.

'Bulongo. Psst,' Jabu whispered and gestured for Kunda to come; as the linen sails separated she momentarily became visible.

Kunda looked around, calculated that he could not be seen and, with the added protection of the stack of linen on his shoulder obscuring his face, side-stepped through the pencil-thin gap, almost catapulting the top layer of whites from his shoulder with the washing line.

A few rows back and advancing, Jabu heard a couple of laundry-women gossiping, laughing and joking. Before Kunda could speak she breathed the name of her friend and where she was staying. In a blink, she ducked out of sight.

Back on the dining deck, which stretched twenty-five feet out into the river to provide unimpeded views along the broad breadth of water in both directions of the channel, Kunda instructed one of the waiters to move a table for two onto the lawn and into the shade of a large fever tree, before sending them both off-duty. He wanted to be able to think. A small house was one thing. More wives, more trouble, and he guessed he had had enough of that already.

oOo

'My husband is a vegetarian.'

The man sitting at the table under the tree was about to speak when his wife, a woman in her mid-thirties, continued abruptly. 'The agent did put it on our booking form, and I'm not eating uncooked meat in this temperature.'

'It is beef carpaccio, madam. It's very popular. Our chef considers it one of his specialities.'

Kunda was about to address the man, who seemed uninterested in the whole affair, his vision cast far out across the river. He moved his head forward slightly as if the added inch or two would make whatever it was he was trying to picture that much clearer.

Suddenly, splashing broke out close to the shrubbery that languished over the edge of the riverbank.

'We're not sitting here.' The woman's chair tipped and clattered as it went over. Her voice was shrill.

'It is perfectly safe, madam.' Kunda spoke to reassure her, as he sprang to rescue the chair.

'We're expected to eat our lunch with crocodiles snapping at our feet. Chuck, say something,' the woman demanded.

Chuck appeared to Kunda to be Mr Average American, who represented almost half of the people he served at the lodge. Not short, not tall, not fat or slim, not dark, not blonde, and his voice not loud or quiet when he spoke.

'Can you please find my wife and I somewhere to sit further away from the water, and different hors d'oeuvres? Without meat.'

Kunda lifted the whole table up into the air above his head and carried it back off the lawn, and under the

149

thatched open-sided canopy. Having re-sat the guests, Kunda walked up the path to reception. The guests' bags had been left in a pile, waiting to be taken to their cottage. Kunda raised his eyebrows and guessed they had come straight to the dining-room on arrival.

'The people just checking in, can I see their booking form?' Kunda addressed the receptionist.

Under 'special requirements', nothing was listed. Kunda walked along the back corridor to the kitchen in the full knowledge that no chef was on duty. All the dishes being cold, the chef had placed them in the fridge at the end of his shift, knowing the waiters could pull each course out when the guests arrived. Kunda could not imagine vegetarian food was that difficult to prepare.

Five minutes later he presented what amounted to two mixed salads with shaved parmesan.

'Where are our drinks?' the woman demanded, without even an eye to her new offering.

'I'll get them now, madam. What would you like?

Lunch did not improve. The starter was pushed aside, the wine was not sufficiently chilled. The entrée, Kunda had been pleased to find, a seafood salad already assembled by the chef, with the ingredients probably flown in from Mozambique, remained only picked-over.

'Ahaaaaaaaaaaaaaaaaa ...' The scream was distant, but Kunda could hear it clearly as he later prepared the buffet table for afternoon tea.

Guests and their guides were beginning to return, hot and weary. The upset that greeted them, Kunda was sure everyone would have heard out across the water.

He saw the boss walking in the direction of the screech which, even from where Kunda was working, he could hear had turned into loud uncontrollable sobbing.

The guides, who held most guests' confidence, tried to assure everyone that it was nothing to be concerned about, having spoken to reception on their walkie-talkies.

Kunda knew the problem without having to ask: it was a dilemma. The boss, who was not normally around in the afternoons, had been summoned.

Ten minutes later, Craig Graves reappeared and approached another couple, who were quietly enjoying tall glasses of homemade lemonade and a selection of open sandwiches, while discussing with their guide what they might plan for the next day.

The shuffling began, an upgrade, an activity normally charged for provided free, all to encourage the newly arrived guests to relinquish their newly acquired horrors. Personal butlers repacked cases, and by the time tea was over all were settled into their new accommodation. The problem guests eyed the Court House not without suspicion: it was set well back from the river edge in a structure converted from what had previously been the tennis court pavilion. Peacefulness assured, as it was surrounded by a high dry-stone wall providing a lush private garden.

Not all concerns had been alleviated, notably those arising from the shadows of the shrubbery. Craig stood waiting for the next volley to be released.

'Anything could be hiding in that foliage.'

The husband, embarrassed and clearly tired, strode around and commenced shaking each of the bushes. Then, bypassing his wife, addressed Craig.

'I'm sorry for all the trouble we've caused. I'm sure this will be very acceptable. Please thank the other guests for agreeing to move.'

Craig breathed a sigh of relief and signalled for the butler to settle them in.

'Not your fault. The agent should have explained the style of accommodation before you booked. Open-fronted cottages on the river bank aren't to everyone's taste, particularly at this time of the season when the water is still really quite high.'

'I think he did, but there was no other availability that fitted in with our safari schedule. And friends of my wife stayed here. They loved it and insisted we included a couple of nights. I don't think my wife quite took it on board.'

'Well, I hope you'll feel relaxed here.' Craig turned and left before another rustle of leaves could be interpreted as a charge of the Big Five.

'When Kunda has a minute, can you ask him to come and see me?'

Craig instructed the receptionist on the way back to his office.

Craig Graves had been described in one of the UK broadsheets as a pillar of the *new British colonials*, the young wealthy who were widely populating Africa. He was profiled as being from a wealthy shipping family, married to a minor minor royal, ex-Gordonstoun and Cambridge, followed by a stint at Stanford and (inaccurately) as related to the poet and novelist Robert Graves.

He leaned back in his chair and wondered whether at the age of thirty-seven, he felt Africa was becoming just a little too much like hard work. He looked at the khaki safari jacket on the coat-stand, which he hated wearing, but it was a piece of attire many of the guests expected. He looked at the vintage hunting rifle hanging on the wall, which had been a gift from a friend of his father who indicated it had come from Hemingway's armoury. 'Still very serviceable: you'll be able to bag a few trophies with that.' It had not left its position since being mounted there twelve years earlier, when the lodge had been constructed.

'Knock, knock.'

Craig snapped back into the current matter.

'Kunda. Come in. Close the door please.'

Kunda assumed the unusual request for the door to be shut, in an environment where doors hardly existed, was so that any guest loitering at reception could not overhear the boss's instructions regarding the guests that had been so disruptive.

'Kunda, I would not normally approach a member of staff on their behaviour away from work. Well, not unless it directly affected the operation here. My wife has convinced me this does. You know how much she concerns herself with the rights of women in this country.'

Kunda fidgeted nervously, not sure where this 'conversation' was heading.

'I have a letter here.' Craig scanned the array of papers spread on his desk. Not seeing the envelope he was seeking, he leaned forward and began to sift, thinking to himself that he really should make the effort to clear some of it down. A clean, crisp manila envelope came into view, at the same moment as an update from an agent caught his eye.

'I'm not sure why this has found its way onto my desk, but maybe you could deal with it.' Craig handed him a fax from an agent, amending a booking instruction: *Please note the gentleman in this pax will require vegetarian meals.*

'And this was given to me yesterday. Please read it.'

Kunda took the envelope and turned to leave.

'Here,' Craig instructed, curtailing Kunda's departure. 'Read it here.'

Kunda laid the fax cautiously on the corner of the table, opened the envelope, and removed two sheets of folded, lined paper. The words were handwritten.

Dear Mr Graves, Sir

I am your hardworking and trusted employee Mr Farai Mubrumbi. I have been working at your fine lodge keeping the buildings in good repair for you and your esteemed guests for seven years. Always I put the needs of my work before my own life.

When I married my wife Jabu four years ago and she moved from her village in the west of this country to be with me here I asked you if it was possible for her to have a job here working for you in this lodge. She was given employment in the laundry where she still works. I was very grateful and thanked you for helping me.

Six weeks ago you requested of me to travel to undertake work at a camp belonging to your friend many miles away and because of the rains and the high waters in the river I stayed away from my wife and my home for a month. I do not complain to you even if this work I do is not work I am paid to do.

When I was away I have found out that my wife Jabu has been to Lusaka with a person working in your lodge enjoying herself with other men dancing and going to parties while I was doing hard honest work for your friend.

I have beaten her and sent her from my house and I now must ask you to sack her as I do not want her to work here at your lodge any more. You provided her with work because she was my wife and I asked you to give her a job. She committed adultery is untrustworthy has brought shame on me so she must leave here.

She was given the job by my asking I now have the right to ask for it to be taken away.

I will always build for you and repair the lodge without complaint and I thank you Mr Graves, God and the Inkanga in taking this bad woman out of my life.

The finest builder in all Africa

Mr Farai Muhrumbi

'I presume you are the person Jabu went to Lusaka with?'

Kunda did not speak. He barely nodded his head, ashamed his philandering had been exposed.

'My wife hears how hard Romance works, and she tells me you are a lucky man to have her as a wife. Frankly, in her opinion, Romance deserves better.'

Kunda shook his head.

'It is not my intention to sack anyone. But I would suggest you keep your zip done up, and give some respect to your wife. Now get back to work, and get your life sorted out.'

Kunda picked up the fax and, without speaking, left the room, head bowed. The next few sullen hours were spent staying out of the way where possible, and snapping at waiters and kitchen staff when forced to confront any inescapable task or duty.

oOo

The woman sobbed uncontrollably. Tears streaked down her face, eye make-up running. She pushed her plate away without looking at it, and took a large gulp of her Chardonnay. Her husband, sitting beside her at the long communal table, put his arm around her shoulder.

'Piss off. Just leave me alone.' The man removed his arm, and the rest of the dozen guests joined in his embarrassment.

The guide hosting the table, equally shocked at the outburst, signalled to Kunda.

'Can you take that away, and maybe ask the kitchen what they can offer that madam may prefer.'

She did not find this consoling: in a single sweep she pushed her cover of plates, glasses, and cutlery off the edge of the table. The smashing sound as it landed on the stone floor echoed across the still water. But the silence that followed drowned out the reverberations, and the lack of continued conversation drew the darkness in around them all.

Her husband leaned closer for a second attempt.

'What are you lot fucking looking at? I hate the lot of you.' The pitch of her second outburst shook off the awkwardness that had briefly held the dinner guests and scrambled a flock of birds in the branches above.

She repelled her husband's overtures immediately with sufficient force that, had it not been for the guest sitting alongside him, he could have joined the broken tableware that one of the waiters was rapidly attempting to clear away.

Standing, almost falling over the kneeling waiter, she looked around the table, her eyes tearing into each of her fellow diners in turn.

Screwing her face into a hideous sneer, she leaned both hands on the table. 'I hate all of you. I hate this place and I hate Africa. I hate it. I hate it.' After spitting the sentiment out, she ran off, out of the arc of candlelight, swallowed up by the night.

The host spoke, because someone needed to: 'I apologize.'

'No, I'm the one who should apologize,' the husband interrupted. 'I'm truly sorry. I've never seen her act this way before. We only flew in this morning. I'm sure she's jet-lagged. But she has been so looking forward to this trip. It was really difficult to keep my diary free to accommodate it.' He spoke quietly, in short sentences, seemingly unable to rationalize his wife's behaviour.

Before anyone could react to what was clearly a pathetic excuse, the woman who had held centre stage with her monologue for the past five minutes returned, lank and silent. She flopped onto a sofa under the open thatch.

Five minutes later, their butler lit the path with a powerful flashlight and escorted the couple back to their cottage. Dinner resumed. The conversation was less focused on the usual sightings and the guide's awe-inspiring tales of encounters in the wild, and regularly reverted to the previous histrionics.

'Who are they?'

'I'm sure I recognize him. I think he was on the cover of Forbes a couple of years ago.'

'Do you know?'

The guide, the soul of discretion, declined any knowledge and tried to continue with what he knew was one of his more popular stories.

'What a terrible woman.'

'Whatever makes someone act like that?'

'Some of the anti-malarials can have very strange side effects. If you've had previous mental problems or you're a little unstable, they can have a psychotic effect. Particularly if you are drinking alcohol at the same time. Not that I'm suggesting that lady has suffered previously.'

'What do you take?' This question was directed to the guide by someone at the other end of the table.

'Most people who live out here don't take anything. I wouldn't want to take any long-term. I think it can seriously affect your liver, apart from one's mental state.'

'What do you do to avoid it?'

'Nothing, really. Long-sleeved shirts and long trousers in the evening, plenty of spray and a mozzy net over the bed. I've had malaria five or six times. You get to know the feeling when it's coming on, and then I'll take some tablets, go to bed, drink lots of flat Coke, plenty of liquid and sugar.'

'Isn't that a bit dangerous?'

'Not many people die of malaria. AIDS is the big killer in this part of the world. I think you'll find that most of the people that have malaria and die are HIV-positive or very badly nourished. Plus, many do not have the money for the tablets. The only real killer, if you're healthy, is if it goes cerebral.'

'What are the government doing about it?

The conversation batted backwards and forwards throughout the remainder of dinner, and later around the fire-pit.

'Doesn't he own executive jets? I'm sure he has a company based in California. No, Texas. Yes, Texas, I'm sure of it.'

The following morning the disruptive couple asked reception to book accommodation at a top international hotel in Cape Town, and first-class flights.

'The earliest I can get a flight to South Africa for you is the day after tomorrow.'

After much telephoning, a frustrated agent in the States persuaded them to accept two nights at the Victoria Falls Hotel in Zimbabwe.

Kunda had not been on the rota for breakfast, which was probably a good thing. At the end of dinner, he had decanted what spirit he thought he could get away with into a single bottle, corked the cocktail, and thrown it over the fence into a bush, hoping it did not fall to the ground and smash on a rock. It was easier than talking and drinking with the guard. He wanted to be on his own.

He parked the car off the main road, on a small patch not visible to any passing traffic. He did not know what sort of trouble could be waiting for him back in the village, and was in no mood to party in the township. He climbed into the back seat, pulled the cork with his teeth, and swilled down three large swallows of the spirit mixture. He needed to think.

His situation with Romance was at an end. She would not forgive him for beating her, and she would not hand over any more of her wages. It was a dream to imagine otherwise. He had known that the time would come when she found out he had spent all the money she thought was saved, but he had pushed it to the back of his mind. He continued to make excuse after excuse why the land they were buying was not available, and the need for her to keep working, just another year. Jabu would have nowhere to live, and would expect to take up with him. She would make his life a misery, with no husband to keep her under control. And then there was her husband.

He could speak to his friends about moving to Lusaka, or to his brother about Jo'burg, but he had never lived anywhere else. The thought of not knowing everyone, having to survive in a big city, unnerved him. He took another swig. With mashed emotions, he slept fitfully and drank a lot, and in the morning he was none the wiser. He would do what he always did. Take each day as it came, and deal with the kak as it floated to the surface. Something would happen, and he knew he just needed to be there to take advantage of it.

Lunch was quiet; all the guests were out; there was only the boss and his wife. Kunda stayed in the background, and also avoided any temptation to venture in the direction of the laundry. He wanted company, but did not want to get caught up spending money on the scarred piece of chicken again. He would go the beer hall after his shift and drink some Mosi with Isaac; maybe there would be some shorty around that would be happy with just a few drinks.

'They know you too well, Bulongo,' Isaac laughed, returning from the bar with three bottles of beer. He placed them on the table and gave Kunda the change. 'She didn't even stay for the beer. That tells you something,' he added, slapping his friend on the shoulder.

Kunda drank the extra beer in two swallows and was not good company after that. He tried to grab each woman that passed, and those out of range he called over. None came, and those that did start pulled away again as they came into reach.

'Relax, Bulonga. You have a good wife and a small house. That should be enough,' Isaac counselled.

Kunda got up for a turn around the hall. When he returned Isaac had gone.

Outside, he smoked some dagga he had been offered by people he knew as they drifted by.

'Hear you got lots of trouble with the shorties.' Kunda offered the smoke back to the guy who had spoken. 'You keep it. I hear her husband is looking for you.'

'He knows where I am.' Kunda got up from the wall he was sitting on and wandered off. Heading nowhere, he stumbled over broken bricks and discarded bottles, shaded his eyes from bright lights that came and went, and bounced from side to side between parked cars. Pitch-dark, in deep shadow … he took a load of abuse from a couple fucking who became disjointed when he barged into them, his apologies going unheard as he turned, retracing his erratic path back in the direction of the beer hall.

'You want go with me?' Kunda knew who it was without looking round to identify the voice from the shadows. He half-fell back into the beer hall, leaned against the wall and counted the few notes in his pocket, all low denomination. Not enough, even if he had the inclination.

He moved swiftly back into the light. At the bar, he caught sight of the Lusaka boys, loud, laughing, a more boisterous crowd than he wanted to be part of.

'Hey, Bulongo. Over here.'

He looked up as though he had not noticed them. They beckoned him. He wasn't even sure he had enough to buy them drinks; he waved and tumbled back out.

'Bulongo, you come fuck me.'

Kunda pushed her away, harder than just a friendly shove.

The Lusaka boys came out an hour later.

'Sha, you blazed?'

'The last chamba I smoke must have been dusted.'

'Lucky man.'

'Sha, you lash me some mahafu.'

160

The short one took a roll of greenbacks from his pocket and peeled off twenty-five US dollars.

'You pay me back two days, before we go back. You don't, I get very flat with you, Bulongo.' He waved the notes in front of him. 'Yes?'

Kunda took the money and walked away without speaking.

'Don't blow it, Bulongo,' the Lusakan called, as Kunda pushed the notes into his pocket.

The following day he did not go to work, using the feverish malarial excuse again.

He did not seek out the inkanga. Their paths had simply crossed.

'Kunda, where are you going?'

Kunda heard the quiet voice drift on the air to him, before he caught the moon glistening on the silver-ringed crook, and then the flap of the white gown.

'Nowhere.' He could not recall if he was on his way somewhere, or had recently left an unknown destination.

'Sit. I invite you to sit with me, Kunda.'

Kunda hovered.

'You are very tight, sha. Sit. I will give you guidance. Do not be afraid. If there are bad things, we can make spells and free you. If we find only good in your future, you can be your usual warried Bulongo.'

As Kunda eased himself up onto a plank, supported by two rust-ridden petrol containers, the witch doctor took his right hand in both hands and felt each of the fingers, then lifted it up to his nose and sniffed the nails. He took the other hand and felt each of these fingers and sniffed these nails. Then, using a small sharp knife, he cut a piece of hair from Kunda's head and massaged it in his fingers.

'Your life is very muddled, Kunda. You should scrub the clunk away and lash back what you have taken. Soon all your trouble will be gone.'

The witch doctor blew the short strands of hair into the

air, then waved a small open bottle he had secreted in his palm under Kunda's nose, before he strapped off into the bush with an assurance that gave Kunda confidence.

Kunda did not know how all his troubles could simply disappear. He contemplated what he needed to change his existence; he was rapidly becoming a joke around the beer hall and the township. And both at work and in the village people were either distant or avoiding him. A year ago he was the man, he had respect. He needed that back, he understood. It would be difficult without the money from Romance, so purchasing his way back would not be easy. He needed a plan. He considered the church but he had not been near the place for a year a more.

Back at work there were two envelopes waiting in the postbag for him.

'Are we going to have sufficient transport tomorrow? It looks as though everyone is heading off in all different directions, and all looking at coming back at different times.'

Kunda could hear the boss in his office talking.

It went quiet for a moment; Kunda guessed he was on the phone.

'I'll go down to the workshop and see if either of the two buggered Defenders can be brought back to life.'

Kunda stuffed the envelopes into his pocket and headed off to the staff boma, wishing to avoid a confrontation about his absence from work.

'You look like kak,' A boatman standing at the fire said, as Kunda approached.

'Thanks.'

Kunda was served a plate of sadza and relish. He sat opposite the boatman at a table, and poured a glass of water.

'You clunk worse than bad kak, man. Take a shower,' the boatman muttered, turning up his nose and going to sit on a large cut trunk of riverine tree fifteen feet away.

Kunda fingered a little sadza into a small ball and dipped it into the thin brown relish. The food in the boma was shit. The staff cook stole ingredients to feed his family, or sell. Kunda knew this for a fact, because on various occasions he had bought meat from him. Normally, he would have waited and eaten from the dining-room food he was able to hold back, but he could not remember the last time he had eaten and his stomach felt as though it was glued to his ribs.

The toilets in the shower block were without seats and blocked. Most staff walked into the bush and took a shit by the fence. They pissed in the showers and the urine collected in pools of soapy water that drained from the cracked ceramic trays. Kunda pushed open one door after another, each time being repelled by the stench and an infestation of flies swarming from their settlements.

The sound of Kunda's palm slapping the ear of the young gardener whose job it was to keep the staff area clean reverberated like the snap from a crocodile.

'It not my fault, Bulongo,' the boy pleaded as Kunda dragged him from the boma and told him to get one of the shower cubicles cleaned.

'The hose is split and the deck scrubber is finished,' the boy protested.

'I come back in ten minutes and I can't get a shower, I'll make you lick it fucking clean.'

'If Farai see you here he will come and beat me.'

Kunda ignored the reference to Farai and picked his way through the bush to the laundry, where he quietly waited; having almost given up when Jabu came out, he signalled her over and, nervously, she responded.

'Get me a pair of black trousers and a white shirt,' he demanded.

Some of the staff paid laundry-girls to do their washing. Jabu had done Kunda's until her affair with him had been exposed.

'There's none of your clothes here, Kunda,' she

explained.

'Clients, staff, there must be some you can find. These need washing. Wash them and I'll bring what you get me back.'

She returned with a pair of black trousers that looked a little short and worn, and a white Ralph Lauren shirt that was still slightly damp. He looked at the logo and decided his jacket would conceal it. He unbuttoned his own shirt and took it off; the armpits were yellow, and stiff with dried sweat. He removed his trousers. Jabu stepped closer, slipped her hand into his shorts and, as he hardened, began to work him. He pushed her away. Then he changed his mind, pulled up the front of her wrap, and fucked her against a tree. When they had finished, Jabu picked up his trousers and the two envelopes Kunda had not opened fell to the ground. She thought about dropping the trousers to conceal them, but before she could Kunda had seen his loss. He stretched out his hand for Jabu to pick them up.

He did not open letters until his shift finished. He ate beef fillet and drank two glasses of sweet white wine in a quiet corner where he could keep an eye out for the prowling accountant. The first envelope he opened made him feel comfortable. A fifty-dollar tip. He would be able to repay the loan, albeit a day or so late. The second envelope he opened did not make him feel comfortable. A small lock of black hair. It looked like his own. The hair that had been blown into the wind.

Later, outside the wire, a voice called to him.

'Bulongo. Here.'

Kunda had not seen him at first; he was off the path, in the dark of the bush. The short sweep of a flashlight gave Kunda a direction. He moved forward, unsure of his reception. He stopped and waited.

'Bulongo. Come,' the voice encouraged.

Kunda remained unsure.

'Kunda, I have something for you. Mahafu.

164

Greenbacks.'

'Who is it. Do I know you?'

'Security man, come on, we must be quick.' The owner of the voice quickly flashed light up on his face for recognition. 'Quick, sha.'

Kunda picked his way through, and pitched forward in the dark as the light from the car park lost power, and at the same moment he pitched again over a large bulk. His hands stretched out to save himself and landed on a body, still warm; a strong smell filled Kunda's nostrils.

'Careful.'

A light flashed down on him and he could see the brown grey waterbuck.

'Fuck.'

'I need you help. Get your car, man. Mine's dead.' The guard spoke quickly now, keen to get the animal away.

'How did you catch that? It's a big bastard.' Kunda's eyes, adjusting a little to the dark, took in the size of the body and then the head, proudly topped with antlers three feet in length.

'Snare. We put out snares. If we're lucky they'll get us a warthog, most of the time nothing. Get your wheels, man. Come on.'

'That won't get in my car.'

'Get your car. I'll cut it.'

'Fuck, there'll be blood everywhere.'

'There's a tarp in my car. It'll be OK. Go, man.'

When Kunda returned, the head had been severed halfway down the neck, and the two back legs hacked off. The guard, soaked in sweat, wielding a logging axe, was splattering blood in all directions.

Four hundred and fifty pounds of dead flesh brought the rear end low enough for the exhaust pipe to hit every rock on the rough track. On the main road, Kunda managed to increase his speed slightly. They were heading away from the township. The guard knew a buyer, but the place where they could find him was on a piece of road Kunda rarely used, and the weight on the springs made the handling difficult.

A truck, lights flashing and horn blasting, tailgated him. The head had been too difficult to fit in the boot but with the security guard insisting it would fetch a good price, they had stashed it on the back seat, only partly covered with branches. Kunda put his foot down without much result; the truck swung to the right and passed them, causing a backdraught that sent Kunda swerving.

A few miles further on the truck was sitting stationary. By the time Kunda could bring his car to a stop it was too late. He was in full view. Quickly he dimmed the lights, and tried to turn without tipping into the deep concrete storm drain. As he began to pull away a loud report from a high-calibre rifle rang out; the bullet penetrated the metal and sank into the already dead meat in the boot.

Kunda knew he could not outrun anything. Another shot took out the back window. He kept his lights off and his foot off the brake. Park rangers were deadly; he had heard only last week that three poachers had been shot dead in a fire-fight. Rangers and police were always setting up roadblocks to catch vehicles transporting game meat without a licence. Kunda's mouth was dry; he wanted to curse, but the vile words would not leave his throat. He put his hand to his shoulder and felt the ooze of warm blood. He flashed his lights quickly; the storm drain only ran along one side of the tarmac. He swung the steering wheel and crashed off the road;, sparks flew as the undercarriage gouged everything larger than the smallest stones. Gravity-powered, Kunda spun the wheel in each direction, trying to regain control.

The rangers, a few minutes behind, did not need the powerful searchlight mounted on the roof of the Discovery. A burst of flame engulfed their prey; setting fire to the tree the vehicle had plunged into provided more than sufficient light. Four of Kunda's pursuers, dressed in dark green uniforms, jumped from the back of the vehicle, slipping the safetys off their automatic weapons as they did so. The team spread out and approached the area of the vehicle in a cautious well-practised manoeuvre.

At daylight, the charred body behind the wheel was cut out. The rangers logged another successful night.

CHAPTER FOURTEEN

The spring dropped out of Stephen's step just as he reached the front door of the office. Sitting directly across the road, parked at the kerb, was the Land Rover that had carted him away months earlier. The shadow of the premises opposite cast darkness over the cab, preventing him from seeing the occupants clearly. But they looked to him like the same team. What he could see clearly was a hand holding a clipboard, and another pointing in his direction.

'Romance, the police are outside. If they come for me, please ring Sanjay immediately. You have his number,' Stephen said, heading directly to his own office without hesitating.

Romance was shocked. Why would they be coming for Stephen, she thought, but could not settle on any viable reason. The first time he had been picked up was after a trip up north; it wasn't long since his return from Mozambique. Romance pondered the coincidence.

No sooner had Stephen disappeared from sight, the front door swung open and four uniformed police officers crowded in, as if seeking to enter all at the same time. Romance began to lift the receiver of her telephone with one hand, and flick through her card index with the other.

At the same time, she opened her mouth to enquire if she could be of assistance. Before she had time to release the words, the officer with some braid on his shoulder spoke.

'Are you Romance? And you have a husband, Kunda, who works in the north of the country?' These were questions to which he already knew the answer, so had little interest in the reply. 'Put the phone down and come with us, please.'

The officer with three stripes on his sleeve eased himself round Romance's desk and took her by the arm, removing a set of cuffs from his belt.

'I don't think that will be necessary for the moment,' the senior officer intervened.

The sergeant applied pressure at Romance's elbow, and firmly pushed her in the direction of the street door, still holding the cuffs in his palm, at the ready.

Despite the imminent possibility of having her hands manacled behind her back, Romance dug her heels in and feigned an authority that she did not have. She knew, in truth, there was little she could do to stop them taking her, if that was their intention.

'If you would like to tell me what you think I've done, we can probably get this misunderstanding sorted out, Colonel.' Romance used the rank, not knowing if it was correct, but knowing that anyone who wore a uniform with braid was not above flattery. 'I have done nothing wrong.'

'Just a talk, Romance. You're not under arrest.' The 'colonel' sought to assure her.

'Well, if she's not under arrest, I don't think it's unreasonable for her to be told what this is all about.' Stephen had come out of his office and joined the group at the front door. As he spoke, he edged his way discreetly between them and the exit. Up close, he recognized three of the men, but the man in charge was not familiar, not the one who had dragged him halfway around the country those months earlier.

Stephen could see they were deciding whether to get heavy-handed or back down. From what he had learned of the police in this country, backing down was not an option normally favoured. He did not want Romance to be on the receiving end of whatever aggressive behaviour they were prepared to hand out. He knew that once it turned nasty, if was difficult to retrieve the situation.

'Gentlemen. Winston, we don't usually see much of you in this part of the country.' Sanjay entered wearing his usual immaculate attire, crease-free and confident. 'So what's this all about? You think this young lady has been supplementing her supermarket shopping with the purchase of a little illicit bushmeat, do you?'

'I'm afraid it is a little more serious than that,' Winston assured.

'Well, whatever the seriousness, I'm sure it's not beyond our joint intellect to get to the bottom of matters without turning this into a major legal battle. Romance, if you would go back into your office.' Sanjay was exercising his natural command of a situation, which no one ever seemed to question.

Romance took a few steps back into her office, separating herself from the group, but leaving the door open so she was not excluded.

'Stephen, if you could give us a few moments. Not wishing to be rude.' Sanjay was politeness itself.

Stephen was pleased to have played his part. He smiled at Sanjay, and discreetly winked at Romance as he extricated himself from the group and returned to his desk.

'After you,' Sanjay gestured the senior police officer towards the recently converted corner that was Romance's office.

Sanjay followed him in, closing the door firmly behind them.

'Romance, please sit. Winnie, so tell us what all this is about, and how it involves this very honest and trustworthy

170

young lady.'

'Well, firstly, I have to inform her ...' Winston's tone and mannerism ignored Romance's actual presence in the room.

Romance listened intently to both men; although one was of Indian origin and the other African, she closed her eyes and their accents were interchangeable. The clarity of a British public school education was unmistakable.

'The lady's husband, Kunda Gwelu, is dead. His death occurred following a car chase in the north of the country, while he was fleeing one of my anti-poaching units who were in hot pursuit. The car he was driving crashed and he died at the scene.'

Involuntarily, Romance put her hand to her mouth and drew breath. She made no other sound or movement.

'I suppose he was shot trying to escape,' Sanjay remarked, knowing the reputation and firepower of the teams recently deployed.

'No. The car hit a tree, burst into flames, and was unapproachable by the time my men arrived. The body was charred beyond recognition. We were able to trace the ownership of the car and obtained a photo of him from his place of work. He was finally identified by a truck driver who overtook the car shortly before the incident. Kunda was confirmed as its driver.'

'Romance, please accept my condolences. May I get you a glass of water? This must have come as a terrible shock.' Sanjay offered his trained empathy.

Romance shook her head. 'No, thank you. I'll be OK.' Her voice was level, her eyes dry. She hoped the uncontrolled shaking she could feel migrating throughout her whole body was not externally visible.

'And why would the death of her husband warrant this young lady being taken into custody?' Sanjay returned swiftly back to business.

'I need to establish if this man was working alone or as

part of an organized poaching ring operating throughout southern Africa. It is possible your client, I presume she is your client, has this information, or may even be part of a chain along which bushmeat, ivory and rhino horn is being trafficked,' Winston elaborated.

'Well, Winnie, as you have said, my client's husband was in the north of the country, not apparently heading in this direction. With the evidence you have, I think it highly unlikely a magistrate would commit this young lady, let alone a jury find against her.'

'That may be the case. But my unit has been achieving notable success, and much of it is due to broadening our investigations well beyond the immediate gang members caught.'

'I'm more than convinced my client will take every opportunity to give you any assistance you require. After you leave, you have my word that I will discuss this matter at some length with her. Should there be any issues arising that I think you should be made aware, I will ensure this information is communicated to you without delay. Now, if I may have a little privacy with my client, and I'm sure she will appreciate time alone to grieve.'

The interview was over. Sanjay ushered Winston to the door and then escorted him and his men out to their car. As he retreated, Romance could still make out the cut-glass tones. 'Winston, I know this woman. She's not the type of person that would be of any interest to you. And, from the impression I've received, the same can't be said of her husband. They recently separated, and she' has been in discussion with me concerning a divorce. But you have my assurance, if I hear anything at all I'll give you a call. Maybe a dinner together sometime. It's been a while.' The two men shook hands, and Sanjay returned to the office.

'Romance, I take it for granted that you did not know anything about any of these activities in which Winston was alleging your husband was involved?'

Romance, still lost for words, gently shook her head and then burst into tears. Sanjay placed his arm on hers, and suggested she take the rest of the day off. Romance felt the warmth of his hand on hers. It was reassuring. She nodded.

'Thank you for stopping them.' Her voice was little more than a whisper. She found a smile for him, and with her other hand lightly squeezed his while it still remained on her arm.

'I'll have a word with Stephen, so he's fully apprised of the situation.'

oOo

Romance remained in her flat for three days. Her grief overrode any guilt concerning the work she knew would be piling up on the desk, the calls that Stephen would not have time to answer, or if he did the length of the list to which they would be added that would be her task to follow up. The expression 'tearing her hair out' had been one she had heard people say, without understanding that it could truly mean just that. She did not literally tear hers but she knew she was close: a form of self-harming, a compulsion to experience a greater hurt than the pain cutting up her insides.

Death, as she had explained to Stephen not many weeks earlier, was a significant part of life in Africa. Her sense of loss was not diminished by the bad turn her relationship with her husband had recently taken. In fact, she believed, in some ways it was made worse. She had so much wanted to heal the wounds that had been given and received, and that had kept them apart.

'Romance.' Stephen's voice from the other side of the door was gentle. 'Is there anything I can get you?'

'No. I just need some time on my own,' she told him, and then heard his steps go quietly away.

After saying thank you to Sanjay, going to her flat and

closing the door behind her, she did something she rarely did. She locked it. Then she sat on her bed, knees pulled up close, arms hugging them tightly. She kept this position, sometimes with her head up, and then occasionally resting her tired forehead on her bare knees. From time to time she turned to look out of the window. It had been dark for many hours before she gave up her position, stood and stretched. She boiled a kettle and made herself a cup of strong tea, which she did not drink.

A list, she decided, she would make a list. But she accomplished no more than tearing a sheet of paper from a pad she kept upstairs to write out to-do lists, reminders, and other thoughts regarding work. Sometimes she would write a shopping list, but generally she used the back of a discarded envelope for that, otherwise she would feel guilty about wasting valuable company stock. It took her a while to find a pen, which confused her, as it was lying where she always left it.

Compiling a list, the first task would be to write to her sister in Jo'burg, if that was where she still was. Maybe she was with Kunda; it had been a long period of silence since her last contact. Maybe it was this item that prevented her from starting the schedule. She knew the risks, and found it difficult to instigate any action that would, in all probability, bring the trouble she found most abhorrent right to her door.

When dawn came she did not turn off the light, unusually for her, and it took a long while for her to realize that she needed to go to the toilet. She had been busting for a pee, even before the police had entered the building the day before. Finally, and mainly to overcome the problem of the first task, she wrote to her sister, asking after her health and for some advice. Then she folded the missive and stood it, no envelope, on a shelf, only partly in view. When she returned the pen to its usual place, she saw she had used all the sheets from the pad, only the grey-brown backing card remaining. The bin was filled with scrunched spheres and finely torn sheets she had discarded in her numerous attempts.

Later, having picked on a few pieces of Nutty Wonders and sipped from a small mug of water to wash down the sweetness of the dates and the dry pieces of pastry that parched her mouth, she reassumed her knee-hugging position, determined not to leave the flat until she had resolved how she would handle the horror she now faced.

The second item on the list she could not prepare, she did not even know she was considering. She had already taken the sheets, those screwed-up but not torn, from the bin, and with the flat of her hand had smoothed out the creases the best she could. She sat down to restart the listing. This proved no less of an obstacle now that it had previously.

With unbearable difficulty she wrote the word *CLEANSING*. She penned each capital letter slowly, and her hand shook so much as she guided the point across the still partly rumpled sheet that it was hardly legible when she sat back and studied it. Stephen had again knocked gently on the door and enquired if there was anything he could do. Again she waited in silence, shuffling her chair slightly to indicate her presence, until his footfall retreated down the hallway.

Another list. Bullet points. Names. The names. The names of each of Kunda's relatives who would line up to exercise their right to cleanse the widow. To rape her. To sexually abuse her with no thought of the consequences, pregnancy, infection, mental or physical hurt. Just one savage violation after another to satisfy ancient tribal tradition.

At the top, she knew, would be Sonkwe. Gentleness was not any part of his nature, not that she had ever encountered. He would pound her, just to exact revenge on her body for the times she had rejected him. The other names never came to be written. The list would have contained seven, maybe eight, had she mustered the courage to put pen to paper. She could see each in turn standing over her, then feeling the full weight and rancid smell of sweat as their bodies pressed her down and they tore at her flesh, molesting her integrity.

Not written, she imagined she could deny their existence. She had to make a decision. She promised herself she would not leave the flat until she had clear in her mind the action she would take. She dwelled for long hours over the woman who had mouthed the hymns in the church pew next to her: the path she had chosen, and how it had ended in what must have been terror. She saw Chipo's face, and understood how the love she must have felt for Kingsley led her to take control of her own fate, to only be with the man she loved. But she could not come to any conclusion for herself.

On the third day, she found her mind wandering. Other things were creeping in. Bits of work. Why had Stephen thought the police were coming for him? Had Kunda really been part of an organized poaching gang? Was the milk in the fridge turning sour? Why did the workers in the yard play their radio so loudly? Had Sanjay's hand lingered on hers longer than was necessary, or had she imagined it? Did Sonkwe already know of his brother's death? Had Kunda's funeral already taken place, or was his body lying unclaimed in a police mortuary?

'Romance, are you sure there's nothing you want, nothing I can get you?' She had heard Stephen's gentle tap, and the growing concern in his voice. She unlocked the door and opened it the smallest fraction.

'I need to shower and change. If you give me an hour I'll be down.'

'It's all right. Just come down when you're ready. Today, tomorrow, next week. Whenever. I was just worried for you.'

'I'll be down soon.' Romance eased the door closed and locked it.

Downstairs Stephen spent a hasty ten minutes putting the place in the best order he could, not wanting Romance to get the impression the business would be in chaos without her. Romance came down an hour later, looking her smartest and giving off an air of efficiency. Just before one, Stephen offered her lunch at the True Zoo, which she refused, continuing to power through every note, file and invoice. Surely the place could not get into this state in just three days.

Stephen was still making himself look kind of busy by the time it reached early evening and Romance was happy to flop into her chair, satisfied she had brought the day-to-day business into a manageable state. She had passed and avoided the stack of files, Kingsley's files, which at various points during the afternoon she had reluctantly added to, but had found no way to reduce.

Kingsley. Chipo. Momentarily her mind hovered over her own dilemma, a dilemma she had still to resolve despite the pledge she had made to herself.

'Well, that was a somewhat manic piece of office hygiene you performed there,' Stephen smiled, as he placed a tall glass of whiskey and lemonade on the desk in front of her. 'I think you've earned that,' he added.

'Tomorrow I must follow up on the appointment of an office junior. If I don't make some headway into Kingsley's files very soon, the whole place will come to a standstill,' Romance replied, without making any gesture towards the glass.

'I thought you would be going back to your village for your husband's funeral,' Stephen said in a low voice, as if the tone of his speech would prevent the words carrying weight and dragging Romance back to a place he could see and understand she did not want to be.

'Kunda has probably already been buried. His family,

what there is of it, will all return and fight over the arrangements. Over the money. My money. It will not be a battle I can win, and it's one that I do not want to fight.' Her voice had a determined strength. She leaned forward and ran her finger down the condensation on the outside of the glass, causing a small puddle of water on the desk, which she immediately regretted. She picked up the drink and took a long sip.

'Thank you, Stephen.'

'Your health.' Stephen raised his glass as he spoke.

Romance smirked. It was tinged with apprehension at the thought, but she did not reply.

o0o

The girl, in her late teens, started just after lunch the following afternoon. The position was viewed as sought-after employment for a girl with no experience, straight from college. Romance set her to work, introducing her to the boss, Mr Simons, showing her the filing, the post, the tea and coffee, and all but scolded her in the art of making sure everything was handled correctly. Later she instructed her in answering the phone, taking messages and greeting people who walked in through the door, customers and tradesmen alike.

By late afternoon Romance had settled herself behind Kingsley's desk, and started the task which she was unsure she would be able to understand, let alone take over or finish.

Stephen had left the office around 5.30 p.m. for sundowners with a client from the Lower Zambezi who was spending a couple of nights visiting a friend's lodge a few miles away. Romance was still trying to fathom out how the costs were calculated when Stephen put his head round the office door some two hours later. 'You don't want to kill yourself,' he almost said, but managed to hold back before the words actually left his mouth.

'Enough is enough, Romance. I'm taking you to dinner. I'm the boss and I'm not taking no for an answer,' he said instead.

In truth, he had drunk one more whiskey than he had intended and would have been equally happy to have made a sandwich at home and had an early night.

Romance did not decline. She was hungry, tired, and felt she could do with the company. She wanted to talk to Stephen about Kingsley's work but did not want to give the impression that it was beyond her. The last thing she wanted was for Stephen to employ a replacement who might end up bossing her around.

'It's difficult. Over time you don't forget someone, but the pain of a death does subside,' Stephen said in an attempt to break awkward silences while they were waiting for their food to be served. Talking had proved less easy than Romance had wished. Out of the office environment, all her personal problems regained centre stage.

'It is not the loss of Kunda that is the problem. Although I will miss him. I know we didn't see each other as much as I would have liked; we were both striving for the same thing. Together.' Romance did not elaborate further.

Stephen waited. The waitress served their food and they ate largely in silence.

After they had finished and the plates had been cleared, both refused anything further. Stephen spoke quietly, looking around as if to assure himself that no one sitting close by was paying too much attention. It was reasonably busy, but even customers sitting at the nearest tables seemed engrossed in their own worlds.

'Is it the cleansing?'

Romance stared at him, but did not answer.

Having spoken the word that was virtually taboo, Stephen decided to blunder on.

'Sanjay explained it to me. After I was released from police custody. It doesn't have to be the way you think.'

'How would you know? You're English, and you're not a woman. This is our custom. It's not something you could ever understand. It's not something most women in this country understand. So don't try and find some way to make me feel good about it.' Romance was talking louder than she realized; she pushed her chair back noisily and walked out. Tears, angry tears, ran down her face.

Stephen caught up with her as she was fumbling with her keys, trying to open the office door.

'I understand,' he said, trying to comfort her, and wishing now he had not broached the subject.

'Stephen, you understand nothing.' Her anger had subsided, and she spoke in a matter-of-fact tone.

The key turned, Romance walked in and Stephen followed her.

'You're right, I don't understand. I don't begin to understand. But when Sanjay explained to me, I researched it. Which I have to say was not easy, and was far from comprehensive. I do believe some headmen have allowed these rights to become a thing of the past since AIDS has become so widespread. Others have agreed for the cleansing to take a more literal aspect: the woman covering herself with mud and having a relative wash it off. Maybe …' He allowed his words to hang in the air. Waiting to gauge Romance's reaction.

'Well, thank you, Stephen. But the headman in my village, like most in the north, is a traditionalist through and through, and if anyone is seen to go against his wishes the local witch doctor is summoned to back him up.'

Stephen put his arm round her shoulder. 'I'm sure there must be some way we can work this out,' he assured her.

'Should I hang myself … like Chipo? Today, tomorrow, Kunda's brother Sonkwe will walk through the door on his way back to the village, and demand I go with him. Then what do I do?'

'I don't know, Romance.' He sat her down, went into his office, and returned with a bottle of whiskey and two glasses. Romance accepted the drink and as she drank from the glass, felt all the energy drain from her. She felt now no better than she did in the first hours after the police had come to arrest her.

'I've been invited up to the Lower Zambezi for a long weekend, leaving on Thursday. Some work, a bit of fishing and a couple of game drives. Why don't you come with me? It'll be … a diversion, and you won't be looking over your shoulder every two minutes, except for the odd lion or two.' He tried to elicit a positive response. 'And it will give you a chance away from here, to think things through. I know you don't believe me, but I'm sure between us we will be able to come up with a plan. What do you say?'

Stephen could immediately see the look on Romance's face.

'Nothing like that. That was not what I meant at all. The Namzami Hide is one of the most beautiful camps on the river. It's just constructed a luxury family tent, two bedrooms, both en suite, and a sitting room. They're looking at putting in a small private pool. Our business could benefit from this sort of development. It was what I was discussing with the owner earlier,' Stephen hurriedly added as validation of his innocent motives.

'I didn't mean that,' Romance said, somewhat embarrassed.

Stephen knew she was lying.

'Tourists come here to see the game, but for many Africans game is a just source of food, or it's vermin raiding livestock on which our farmers depend. Many see it very differently.'

'Are you telling me you've never been on a game drive? It's a great experience, I promise you. You should come anyway, even if it doesn't give the opportunity to solve all your problems.' Stephen had an excitement in his voice that was somehow infectious.

o0o

The single-engined aircraft bounced along the dirt runway, and began to noticeably brake in order to cut its speed. Through the small triangular window, there was nothing, or nothing Romance would normally associate with an airport. A red fire extinguisher, hooked to a tree, flashed past. And she thought she saw the stripes of a zebra, but could not be sure.

The flight had been quite exhilarating at times, but mostly scary and very bumpy. Whether this was normal or not she could not decide, not having flown in any type of aircraft before. Was it usual for the pilot to spend so much time reading the paper?

'You'll find a copy of the *Daily Express* tucked behind your seat, if you could pass it over,' the pilot had requested just after take-off. 'I've requested clearance to climb five thousand feet, but Lusaka tower has refused, so you might find it a little turbulent down the line. Nothing to worry about. There's bags in the back of the seats if you feel sick.'

Romance turned and looked at Stephen, who was crushed into the space next to her. He smiled, but she was not sure the reassurance on his lips extended to his eyes. She held the arm of the seat sufficient to turn her knuckles white, and although tempted to take a sick bag she maintained control of her small-portioned sadza breakfast.

'Vaughan's doing well,' the pilot informed them as he finished reading the cricket and folded the paper. Yesterday's, if you're interested; picked it up in Lusaka this morning.' He handed the paper to Stephen. 'The weather down there's quite clear; we're just coming back over the Zambezi. If you look out of the window you should be able to spot a fair amount of game.'

With that he banked to one side and flew low, allowing his passengers to see a large herd of elephant and then, further on, water buffalo by the hundred. Stephen touched Romance's arm, pointing to a sandbank in the middle of the river. They were low enough to see half a dozen crocs slide off the sand into the water. Romance felt herself visibly tremble.

A game-viewing Land Rover pulled up alongside the plane as it drew to a halt. Digby stood up and hopped out before either vehicle had come to a halt. He was a good client of the business, having two houses in the town, both with large swimming pools, and was now considering installing one at Namzami, if he could entice the National Park Authority to allow a semi-permanent construction. He always reminded Stephen of a slimmer Lord Lucan, although considerably younger. He guessed the moustache added to the image, which he thought Digby possibly played on. Did guests speculate behind his back whether he was the long-lost infamous English lord, sought by Scotland Yard for killing his children's nanny. Stephen would not have been surprised.

'We had to chase some wild dog off the runway just before you landed. If we're lucky they might still be around. The drive will take just over an hour. Mike is our driver, he has some soft drinks, oranges and cold towels in the chill box. If anyone needs to pee, there are plenty of bushes to go behind. It's a fairly bumpy drive so be warned, but you should get to see plenty of game,' Digby said in his incisive English accent.

'You worked with Kingsley, I hear,' Mike said, offering a soft to Romance. The thought was welcome, but her need to go to the toilet prevented her accepting. The idea of crouching down behind a bush while the three men waited for her was something she wanted to avoid. 'We were at school together,' Mike added.

'How was the flight? I didn't realize you were bringing a

friend.'

Stephen and the camp owner were standing together a few yards from Mike and Romance.

'Romance is a friend, but not in the sense you mean. She virtually runs the office and she's been through a bit of a hard time recently, so I suggested she come. Did try to call you on the sat, but ...' Stephen let his reply tail off; everyone understood the difficulties with communications in this part of Africa.

'No problem: as I said, you have our new family tent. Plenty of space. Did she go on the manifest?

'No. The pilot said to get the paperwork changed would take all day. So he just told Romance to keep her head down when we taxied passed the tower. Was that OK?'

'Yeah. Nobody down there knows what they're doing. I send a list of guest names and the OK comes back three weeks after they've gone. Does she have a passport?'

'No, just ID papers.'

'Fine. The pilot's a good man. He's not going to say anything. Cause himself trouble. Not going to do that.'

'Does he always read the paper when he's flying? It's a bit unnerving.'

'He could take off and land with his eyes closed. One of the few whites that flew for Mugabe's lot out of Mozambique during the war. Not so sure he would have if he'd realized how things would turn out, mind you. I think he'll chuck it in soon. Keeps saying the whole of this part of Africa is finished. I know he's been looking at setting up some flying thing in Kenya.'

'Digby. Stephen here forgot to introduce us.' He extended a coarse hand to Romance. 'Welcome to the Lower Zambezi.'

Like an eager tourist, Stephen climbed into the raised seats behind Digby and Mike, offering a hand-up to the reluctantly intrigued Romance. The Land Rover climbed towards the flat area of hard ground where the trees were starting lose their leaves. The escarpment had felt quite open, and they had stood keenly scoping the landscape in the hope of catching sight of the wild dogs, but without success.

A mile or two on they had dropped down and as they did so the bush had thickened, the tracks became narrower and the sun was blocked by thick dark trunks and green shadowed leaves hanging like huge dreadlocks.

Stephen clicked off half a roll of film when fifty yards to their right a herd of elephant with their young came into view.

Later, Mike brought the vehicle to a gentle stop on a narrow bend, then slowly reversed ten yards. A huge lone male elephant lolloped around the corner in front of them. Both Romance's and Stephen's hands, simultaneously white-knuckle gripped the metal frame on which the canvas sunshade was stretched.

'He'll be fine if we just sit tight,' Digby assured them.

Romance thought by this Digby meant that it would turn and wander off, but instead it continued moving towards them, finally stopping with its trunk touching the Land Rover grille. Neither moved.

Digby turned his head and spoke softly.

'That strong smell you can smell means he's in musk.'

As Digby turned back, the elephant moved to one side, calmly flattening the bush as he progressed along the side of the Land Rover. Romance moved her hand and lightly allowed her fingers to touch the grey skin of the animal that was now dwarfing them. She was surprised at how un-rough it felt. And equally surprised that she had actually touched it.

Moments later both parties were back on their respective ways.

Over the next ten miles, every few minutes Digby continued to spot a broad assortment of bird and wildlife, some in small groups, others alone. At one point in the far distance they saw another Land Rover, but humans seemed to be in the definite minority.

'Over there, under the tree,' Mike said, bringing the pace to a crawl, before stopping close to three lions stretched out, bellies bloated.

'They were on a kill as we drove over to pick you up. The male, the one with the mane, is Nelson. He's only got one eye. Lost the other in a fight, five or six years ago.'

They watched them for a while, Nelson lifting his head a couple of times to lazily survey his surroundings and consider if the new arrivals disrupting his sleep were any threat.

Dinner had just been Stephen, Romance, Digby and his wife. Two other couples staying at the camp had both chosen not to dine at the host's table. The honeymooners had taken the opportunity to have a candlelit dinner served on a platform floating in the river; waiters ferrying food and drink by canoe. The other couple, wishing to keep their celebrity status as private as possible, had elected to have all their meals served on the decking in front of their tent.

After dinner, Digby insisted everyone had a brandy around the fire-pit before retiring. Romance sipped her drink, which proved to half fill the small balloon. She disliked Digby's wife immediately, surprised at the way she openly criticized the staff working there and the insecurity she felt when Digby was out of camp. Digby, Romance liked, enjoying his stories, told one after another to entertain his guests. How, she wondered, did two people with such different attitudes come to be together.

Suddenly, Romance knew she could not drink anymore and that it was time to go to bed. Moving her chair slightly back into the darkness, out of the light provided by the flickering embers of the logs, she discreetly poured most of the dark liquid from her glass onto the grass.

'I'll get one of the guides to escort you back. We don't allow guests to walk on their own after dark.' Digby picked up a radio. Moments later, a park ranger arrived with a rifle slung over his shoulder and a Maglite in his hand.

'I might as well call it a day too,' Stephen volunteered.

'If you have any washing, your butler will pick it up in the morning, but rinse out your own panties, Romance. You don't know what those boys in the laundry get up to – or maybe you do,' Digby's wife warned, with more than a hint of nastiness in her tone.

Both Romance and Stephen saw Digby give his wife a disapproving stare.

Romance's instinct was to ignore the advice; she did not feel inclined to side with the woman she found more obnoxious by the minute, but decided that any rebuff would give rise to an unspoken conclusion that she was siding with her own.

'I'm used to doing my own washing, so it won't be a chore,' she replied with a smile.

Digby's wife picked up the brandy bottle and splashed a considerable amount of liquid into her glass, her duty for the evening done.

The ranger, Romance and Stephen walked the hundred and fifty yards in single file to their tent. On three occasions their chaperone brought the column to a halt, listening to a rustle in the bush close by. But then, confident they were not about to be charged, they moved quietly forward.

The tent was erected in a cleared area of bush, looking out over the Zambezi to the front and with a shallow inlet to the side. As they approached, turning off the path towards the entrance, the ranger stopped and waved his two followers to his side. Between them and the entrance to the tent, a hippo, that could have been mistaken for a large dark shadow, stood grazing.

'We can't risk trying to get past him. Squat down and hopefully it will move off before too long.'

Twenty minutes, which to Romance felt like an hour, passed with little movement.

'We'll go back a little and see if we can approach from the other side,' the ranger suggested.

They proceeded along the path running parallel to the back of the tent. But this was cut into the bush only as far as the staff needed to go to top up the tent's gravity water tank. Easing round to the front from there would have brought them directly to the point where they had last seen the hippo. The ranger, using a machete, extended the difficult path around to the far side of the tent. Stephen's hand hovered over Romance's shoulder, as much to reassure her as to ensure he was stepping in her footsteps. They reached the bank of the inlet, where the water was still quite high and the muddy edge was broken down in places where water buffalo had trampled through.

'We'll have to turn back,' the ranger announced, Romance and Stephen almost falling backwards into the uncleared bush as they made way for the man to take lead position again.

Back at their original position, the ranger scanned the bush to locate the hippo, who had apparently moved away.

'It looks as though he's gone. Once you're inside, close the flaps and you will be very safe,' the ranger assured them.

Before they had walked half a dozen steps and the ranger had finished talking, the hippo came crashing out into the open from the bush, close to the inlet. The ranger shouted, threw up his arms, and pushed Stephen and Romance behind a thicket of trees.

The hippo slowed, stopped with a judder and resumed grazing in an area close to where they had first spotted him.

Another twenty minutes passed and the hippo, apparently content with the extent of his menu, remained conscientiously grazing.

'I think we'll have to go back to the dining area and wait in comfort. I will get you some drinks. Maybe we'll need to organize an alternative tent for you both.' The ranger capitulated.

They trudged back to the apparent safety of the dining area, tired of having to wait so long and still not having been able to get to their accommodation. Romance and Stephen stood by the dying embers of the fire, while the unknown splashed violently in the river close to the bank.

'People pay large amounts of money for all this. I think I would prefer to spend mine at the Victoria Falls Hotel,' Romance commented, waiting nervously to see what would happen next.

'Hippo causing you a bit of difficulty, I hear,' Digby said, marching towards them from out of the dark. 'See if we can't get you in there using the Land Rover. By the way, apologies for my wife: she gets a bit stressed spending long periods in the bush. Doesn't really like it. Thinks all sorts of rubbish about the staff being all male. But you let women work here, and next thing you know everyone's fighting over them.'

A few minutes later they were reversing back down the path with Digby looking back over his shoulder, steering cautiously to avoid the overhanging branches and the holes on either side. Swinging left, Digby brought them to a halt and waited to gauge the reaction of the hippo.

'Why are we reversing?' Stephen whispered.

'If he decides to make a charge I don't want to be looking to do a three-point turn.' Stephen could just make out the wry smile on Digby's face as he had replied.

Digby edged back a few feet and waited. The hippo eyed the intruder, snorted and bundled off, crashing through the bush as it went.

'Some of the rangers are over-cautious, but your man has lived in a local village here all his life; if he says it's not worth the risk, it's not worth the risk,' Digby said, then wished them both goodnight.

Romance refused a drink, said goodnight to Stephen and went to her room. Moments later she came out.

'Someone's been in here. All my things have been taken

out of my bag,' she said, as much embarrassed by the thought that someone had been able to inspect the few possessions she had bought for the trip, mainly in the market, than the possibility that anything had been stolen.

'It will have been the butler. He unpacked my stuff too. It's all part of the service,' Stephen assured her.

She returned to her room, not sure how she felt about having a man go through her more personal items, particularly after the verbal attack on the staff Digby's wife had made at the fire-pit.

Stephen poured himself a beer from the mini-bar and sat on the sofa in the dark, looking out through the mosquito netting, across the river towards Zimbabwe. The moonlight provided everything with the familiar metallic coating. Stephen could make out pin-points of white light from lamps mounted on the canoes of fishermen luring in their catch.

He glugged down the last mouthful of the cold liquid, stood up, with the intention of getting a second, when his gaze was drawn to a sliver of light from a narrow crack between the canvas flaps of Romance's room. He looked away and knocked the top off another Lion. As he returned to the sofa, a slight breeze he had felt a moment earlier opened the gap a few more inches. Romance walked across the bedroom and stood naked in front of the mirror.

Stephen felt guilty watching her silhouette, but his feet did not move and his eyes remained transfixed. She stood in his gaze for only a moment, turned, looked up into the darkness at him, but not seeing him, and slipped unclothed under the crisp white duvet before turning out the light. He wondered if she always slept in the nude.

Moments later, his beer finished, naked Stephen slipped under the sheets. He ran his eyes over her small curved back, down over her round cheeks, where they joined her thighs but were not part of them. The nipple-capped rise of her breasts, the small swell of her stomach gently receding as it tapered down to an intensely dark triangle she exposed as she'd turned. He felt his penis harden as he revisited the images. Had she seen him? Had her nakedness been an invitation for him to go to her? He could not decide as his mind brought them together. The last thing he remembered before falling into an unsettled sleep was a distant bang, which he thought was coming from deep in the bush, but could just as easily have been echoing across the river.

'Knock knock … Knock knock.' The butler's voice mimicked the sound of a clenched fist on a solid wooden door. 'Please come quickly.'

'What?' Stephen replied, roused only slightly from a deep sleep.

'Please come quickly. Mr Digby sent me to get you.'

'I'll get a shower and I'll be right there. Ten minutes.'

'Please come straight away. Mr Digby said it was urgent. To come straight away,' the butler implored.

Stephen swung his legs out of bed, his feet landing on a pile of still wet tissues. He dropped them in the bin in the bathroom, threw some water over his face and pulled on the longs and shirt he had been wearing the night before. Romance was standing by the sofa wearing a flowered housecoat. He did not register her presence when he emerged.

'What's happening?' she asked, seeming to be more awake than Stephen.

'I don't know. It would appear Digby wants to talk to me. I'll be back shortly.'

'Sorry to rush you, old fella – Christ, you look as if you've been up half the night.' Stephen could feel Digby searching his face for clues as he spoke.

'No. Very quiet night. What's the problem?' Stephen asked.

'Mr Johal, your solicitor, is on the sat-phone. It sounded important. And you know what the connection is like round here.' Digby led Stephen to the open-sided tent that served as an office.

'Sanjay, what's the problem?' Stephen could hear his own voice coming back to him down the line.

'They think they've tied Romance into the poaching ring. They know she's down in the Lower Zambezi and there's been a big anti-poaching push in that area over the past couple of days. Past couple of days. Days. Can you still hear me?'

'Yes. There's some echo on the line but I can hear OK,' Stephen said.

'I received a call from a contact at the police station a couple of hours ago. They're saying Romance heard of the raids and went down there to warn the gang. Rubbish, of course. I presume she's with you?'

'Well, she's at the camp,' Stephen confirmed.

'They intend to pick her up at the airport when she returns, and they'll probably arrest you and the pilot for not declaring her on the manifest.'

'How did they know?'

'It seems they called at the office to ask Romance something incidental about her husband, and the young girl who was tidying up unlocked the door and told them where she had gone. When they checked the flight details Romance wasn't listed.'

'It was last-minute,' Stephen explained.

'My suggestion is that you get her on an inbound flight at Lusaka. Something that's stopped over from London or somewhere outside Africa. They won't be looking for her on a long haul. Then you fly back with everything in order.'

'Will that work?' Stephen was fully awake now. The thought of being hauled off to gaol again pumped adrenalin through his veins.

'Don't see why not, and neither of you will be breaking any laws. Does she have a passport?'

'No, just ID papers.' Stephen's voice hesitated, already seeing their plan faltering.

'When she's got a flight, let me know the number and I'll be at this end to meet her.'

'Sanjay, you're a lifesaver.'

'Do not worry. But don't choke on my bill when it arrives.'

The line went dead.

'Problem?'

'I need to get Romance to Lusaka,' Stephen replied, his brain working overtime to take in the reality of the situation Sanjay had just conveyed.

'Bit of a bumpy trip, but she can go out overland. No problem, I can send Mike with her.'

'Yes, that would be good. Thanks, Digby. It really is quite important.'

'As I said, no problem. What's the trouble, has she had a death in the family. Happens all the time out here.'

'Well, she has, but that's not the problem at the moment. Her husband was killed transporting illegal bushmeat and the police are trying to say Romance was part of the gang, or some such nonsense. They know she flew down here, or rather they think they know. Supposedly to warn some poachers down here. Sanjay wants me to fly her back on an international inbound. Throw them off the scent.'

'Best not go overland then. There was shooting last night. The anti-poaching unit won't be far away. Best she goes by river. Stick close to the Zim border. The Zims don't like it, but really there's bugger-all they can do about it.'

Romance sat on the sofa, wondering how her life had suddenly taken this terrible turn. It was only a few weeks ago she believed she was doing OK. Better than OK. In control of her future. Then the argument over money, Kunda storming off, his death, the cleansing, and now the police.

'What next?' She spoke her thought out loud.

Stephen bent forward and took her tea out of her hand. Soon there would be more in the saucer than the cup.

'Digby is arranging for you to go to Lusaka by boat. Up the river, and then a shortish drive into the city. Mike, the guide that picked us up at the airstrip, is going to go with you. He seems fine, and Digby trusts him.'

'He went to school with Kingsley,' Romance said.

Stephen could not decide if this last comment was in support or the reverse.

'I hate the idea of being on the river.'

'There's nothing to worry about. I'll come with you if it makes you feel happier.'

Romance held Stephen's hand as she stepped unsteadily from the bank out across the gap. When she had gained her balance she let go, and as instructed sat centrally on the bench seat.

The boat was a small Boston Whaler, with an outboard Stephen considered a couple of sizes too inferior for the hour-and-a-half journey it turned out they were undertaking.

'Sorry it's not a 500, but import allocations in this part of the world are really restrictive,' Digby explained as the boatman pulled the starter cord. Lucky to be reaching the road by nightfall, but important they did. Then an overnight stop in Chirundu. That was the intention.

'Here's a letter to our ground handler at the airport. Mike will drop her there and our man will arrange the flight and make sure she gets away all right. I'll see you late tomorrow,' Digby said, handing Stephen the envelope.

'Thanks.'

'Oh, and don't let the boatman persuade you to stop off at his village. It's close to the river. He'll get pissed and you won't see him for days. I've been on the sat and booked you some accommodation'

At the first bend in the river, the boatman reluctantly took Mike's instruction and steered towards the far bank, crossing the border, which was a notional line running along the centre. Stephen guessed the reluctance was less due to any fear of the Zimbabwean authorities, and more to do with the distance put between the route and the location of his village, wife and children, as Digby had predicted.

Both sides of the bank were heavy with foliage. They passed the occasional canoe and one lodge craft heading midstream in the opposite direction, which offered a hello with a short blast on its horn.

Nobody spoke much, each in their own little world surrounded by the relentless drone of the engine. From time to time Mike pointed out elephant, buffalo or kudu coming down to the river to drink, baboons swinging noisily from tree to tree, and a white-headed fish eagle sitting among high branches, staring down for signs of prey. After a while, the crocs and hippos in countless numbers failed to gain recognition.

One hour into the journey, nothing seemed to have changed. If Dennis Hopper had appeared on the bank with a spaghetti junction of cameras hanging around his neck and waving his arms, Stephen would not have been surprised.

'Something about not getting out of the boat, unless you were prepared to go all the way. Absolutely bloody right!' Stephen must have mumbled Willard's misquote aloud.

He shook his head in response to the turn of heads, querying his comment. He deliberated if he was prepared to get out of the boat, if he was prepared to go all the way. Had he already, just by helping Romance? He wondered if that was the way the authorities would see it, if he was caught at any point.

'Lots of "ifs" there,' he mumbled, but this time no one looked up.

They tied up at the hotel jetty at least an hour before sunset. Romance was reluctant to leave. Stephen gave her a big hug and waved goodbye as she sped off towards the main road in the pickup Digby kept in the hotel car park.

Checked in and stretched out on the bed, his body was still vibrating from the continuous shudder of the boat. An hour and forty minutes that felt like four hours. He considered Romance's departure. The hug. It had seemed a natural thing to do. Romance had not pulled away as he had taken hold of her. It was the first time they had made more physical contact than a shake of hands when they were first introduced, and the brush of skin when handing over a file or a cup of tea, and somehow when he put his arm round to console her on the news of Kunda's death it was without physical feelings. The holding of her hand earlier in the day went unlisted. He thought of the fleeting glance of her standing unclothed the night before. Held in his arms, her body had felt different from the way he had imagined it might. The phone rang. It was reception, enquiring if he would be wanting dinner this evening.

CHAPTER FIFTEEN

He was scared. He was a different person when he was this
scared. The crash had jarred his shoulders, gashed his
eyebrow, and scrambling out onto the ground he had badly
grazed both shins. Money was a problem. He could not
return to the lodge, the village or the township, without
arousing attention. The police were bound to be snooping
around all his known haunts. He wondered how long it
would be before they realized the deception. He was sure
that the security guard was dead before he pulled him onto
the driver's side, but witnessing the explosion of the petrol
tank and the raging fire that engulfed the vehicle, Kunda
was sure it would take them time. Maybe if he was lucky,
quite a long time.

First he had headed away from the river and the main
road. He'd found somewhere to sleep, but the fear that he
was being tracked and the thought of being trampled on or
bitten kept him semi-awake most of the time, ears alert,
monitoring each rustle and twig-snap.

He got up aching more than when he had laid down,
only now he was cold and thirsty. He looked at himself, and
was not encouraged by what he saw. Dirt on his clothes and
skin, crumpled shirt and trousers, scuffed shoes, and blood.

More blood than could come from someone who had not suffered a fatal injury. Blood that had pooled in the tarpaulin wrapped around the beast had cascaded over him as the car had come to its severe halt at the base of the hit tree.

Kunda decided to head further north, staying in the bush until he came across somewhere he could steal clothes and food. There were small dwellings, clusters of a few thatched huts dotted about all over the place. The owners worked the land and kept a few animals. He felt sure he would pass some during the day, where he could try to steal a little from each so as not to arouse too much suspicion.

It was a plan that, after an hour of trying to pick his way through areas of dense vegetation, he abandoned. Angry, he kicked out at the leaves and branches around him, and then sat on his haunches. He felt wretched. He needed Romance. She had money. She could make a plan. He was sure she still loved him, he could word her up. They could both go down to Jo'burg. Start again. He had fifty US dollars and some local that had been in the security guard's wallet which he had taken in a flash, but an instant that could have cost him his life. More than enough for a ticket. But on the bus there was always the chance of meeting someone he knew, there was nowhere to hide. It would take forever to walk. It wasn't even his fault. His brain was fuzzy. He needed to think straight. He didn't even know if his plan had worked. Did everyone think it was him that was burnt to death in the car? He didn't even know why he had done it. Spur of the moment. Think. Think.

What was most important? Clean clothes, some food and something to drink.

Kunda changed direction; hobbling, with aching limbs and the pain of hunger in his belly, he headed back. Risking any possible patrols, he kept the cover of the bush but skirted along the main highway, heading for the township. After dark, he had decided he would go to the little scar-

faced prostitute. Christ, he couldn't even remember her
name. She would have food, and he could send her out to
buy him a shirt and a pair of jeans. He could pay her. If he
paid her she would keep quiet. He would threaten to beat
her if she told anyone. Then maybe he could get a lift down
to Romance with a trucker.

By late afternoon Kunda had walked past the turn off to
the village. He had thought about taking it and going to
Jabu, but he didn't trust her. The road was busy. While he
rested, squatting out of sight, he thought he saw Isaac's
pickup go by. He could go to Isaac, but he knew if there
was any doubt that he wasn't dead Isaac would be watched.
If he did anything out of normal routine, they would be
onto him. He didn't want to bring his friend trouble.

Kunda walked the last part slower than he had intended,
and it was already dark by the time the lights of the
township were opposite him. He had no energy. He decided
he would have killed for a bowl of sadza. It was eleven
o'clock by the time he felt sufficiently confident to cross the
road, by which time most people were either inside their
homes or the beer hall. Those who were out were minding
their own business.

Kunda found some empty cardboard boxes dumped
next to a bin, and carried these to obscure some of the
blood in case he walked directly into someone. He walked
upright, but kept his head bent. The way he was limping, he
thought it unlikely anyone would recognize him from a
distance.

Outside the girl's door, he waited and listened. There
was no sound from inside. He tapped gently. There was no
reply. A group carrying bottles and talking loudly walked
through a pool of light along the street shining out from the
open door, and turned in his direction. Kunda pushed the
door firmly with his shoulder and it swung open. He
stepped in and closed it behind him. At that moment,
relieved in the safety of the enclosed, he relaxed his aching

muscles. He dropped the boxes and fell back against the door. He heard the party outside pass by. Nobody had taken any notice. He breathed out a further release of tension, stood upright, stacked the boxes out of the way, and went in search of food.

He sat at the table, eating relish that had been left in a pan from an earlier meal. He didn't know what it tasted of and did not care. She always had beer for her guests, and the two bottles he downed in quick succession masked any flavour.

He realized there was no need for her to see the blood on his clothes at all. And that her not being here was his first piece of luck. He stripped to his shorts and rolled everything else up. After he washed, he hid the bundle away in one of the boxes.

Outside there were voices again. Kunda quickly plunged the room into darkness, and grabbed the pan from the kitchen table. There was a man talking. Kunda wanted to cough, but managed to control the urge. The door opened.

'I think someone's been in here,' he heard the girl say.

As she looked to restore the light, Kunda stepped forward and swung the pan hard at the man's head. As the two connected the hollow cracking sound echoed round the walls, and the man crumpled. The scream from the girl died in her throat as Kunda powered the fist from his other hand squarely into her face, sending her unconscious to the floor.

Think quickly. He knew if things were not to go badly wrong he needed to think quickly.

He secured the door. He knelt next to the man. He could hear heavy breathing. The man was not moving. He felt for a pulse. The man was dead. The heavy breathing was his own.

'Fuck, fuck, fuck.' His upper teeth bit harder into his lower lip at each attempt to hold the obscenity to a whisper.

He crossed the floor. The girl's breathing was shallow.

In the back of his head he wished she was dead. Somehow that would have taken the options out of the equation. Killing the man had been easy: it was unintentional. Kunda took a large kitchen knife and slashed the girl's already scarred face; she reacted violently. He then plunged it into her stomach. Blood oozed dark onto the floor. Vomit filled his mouth. He was weaker now than at any time previously. The sour beer-tasting liquid he held and swallowed back. He took his rolled-up clothes, bloodied them with the fresh pool forming on the kitchen floor, and dropped them close by.

Walking back to the highway, he went over everything he had done to check he had not forgotten any detail before running back was no longer possible. His final action had been to wrap the girl's hand around the handle of the pan, strip the man to his shorts, and put the kitchen knife in his hand. He knew if the picture was right the police would not investigate too deeply. Prostitute is attacked by her client, she fights back and both end up dead. It happens. Write a report. End of story.

It seemed more trucks were travelling northwards that night. He contemplated the possibility of heading south, hiding out in Romance's apartment, but it was too risky. If she just disappeared, he knew it would look suspicious. He knew he would be able to trust his brother, if they travelled as far as Jo'burg, but he could not rely on Prudence to keep her mouth shut. He did not know why, but Romance's sister had always hated him.

Ignoring the saloons and pickups, he thumbed each truck as it passed. The clothes he had taken from the dead man weren't perfect, he had been a little bigger, but with the shirt tucked in and a turn-up on the trousers, Kunda didn't look much different from most people.

The seventh truck pulled over. Kunda coughed on the dust as he ran to where it had stopped. He opened the door and climbed up.

'Lusaka?' Kunda asked.

'Get in.'

Kunda swung himself into the seat. The driver was white with no hair, no neck and large ginger freckles covering his face. Somehow he reminded Kunda of a pig.

'You have to pay if you want me t'take you all the way.'

Kunda took a ten-dollar note from his pocket and handed it to the pig.

'And another. Tens too small.'

Begrudgingly Kunda passed over a second note, which the driver pocketed before pushing the lever into 'drive'. Another cloud of dust plumed as his wheels left the verge, rejoining the tarmac and traffic heading north. Both men sat silently for the first twenty-five miles. Nursing only a fear of anti-poaching roadblocks, Kunda fell asleep, staring into the darkness ahead.

The trucker had dropped him well outside the city limits. Although Kunda had paid money for the ride, he did not feel he could demand to be taken all the way. When the truck had stopped to have its papers checked, the driver had bundled him into the footwell and told him to keep his mouth shut. Kunda did not know why the man would help him, and he was a miserable bastard for sure, but Kunda was grateful.

Kunda walked into the centre of Lusaka, tired and hot, but with a feeling that he had escaped not only the evils he had committed, but the need to be in constant hiding, constantly aware, and even his guilt.

It was mid-morning, but on which day Kunda was not aware. His watch told the time, but not the day or date. It was a good timekeeper which he had bought from one of the housemaids years ago. He guessed it had been 'lost' by a guest. Looking at it now, the strap was scuffed, the glass scratched, and the wrist to which it was fixed was gouged in lines with dried blood from where he had pushed his way through the undergrowth, however many nights earlier. He was looking at it not to see the time, but in the realization it was the only thing of any probable value he could now lay claim to. Nausea swept away the moments of euphoria.

oOo

'Hey, Bulongo, you look as if you strap all the way from the Falls. Zimbabwe look better than you.'

Kunda was not sure coming here was a good idea. The team had turned up at the township, so he knew they could at any time return there and it was possible someone would mention he had been killed. But he also knew he could not survive very long completely on his own, and these tsotsis seemed to be his best chance. Thugs were no friends of the police, they could keep their mouths shut. He was not sure if living the life of a gangster was what he wanted, but he had decided to get in with them for a while. Maybe make enough to buy his way out of Africa.

'They all gone drinking, man. Find some clothes that don't clunk and we'll go down Cairo Road. See if we can't word up a shorty. Find a nice lady for you. Put a smile on your ugly face.'

Kunda did not know the name of the young man he was talking to, but recognized his face well enough.

'In there. In there. He's your size.' The man pointed to a curtained hanging space. The clothes were mainly expensive designer labels, far beyond the quality of anything else surrounding him. Empty cans, glasses filled with discarded cigarettes, bare hard dirt floors with pieces of damaged lino, and a bed that looked and smelled as if an animal had recently vacated it. Kunda took the two oldest pieces of clothing, anticipating the owner might not feel as benevolent as the guy in the other room now rolling a joint in a piece of brown paper, having already drenched himself in a pungent aftershave.

Kunda climbed into the bakkie, the tyres screeching on

203

the dust road before he had time to close the door.

They pulled up in the car park of the Brightwater Hotel an hour later, having made three stops on the way. Kunda had watched as the driver jumped out each time and disappeared into a crowd or down a side street, returning a few minutes later without any expression on his face.

He had tried to work out what the driver was doing but couldn't. The driver jumped back in, slapped him on the knee, flashed a grin and screeched off. Kunda knew better than to ask. With tsotsi it was best not to be too inquisitive.

'This is Bulongo. Move over, girls.' The women shuffled round the booth. They had looked bored. The bar was empty, except for three Chinese in dark suits sitting at a table at the other end, drinking water and passing sheets of typed paper backwards and forwards. Kunda could see the little money he had could quickly disappear if they made an afternoon of it. The driver waved to the barman.

'Five whiskies.'

Kunda guessed the women had been drinking straight Coke. Their faces assumed smiles, and the one sitting next to Kunda slid back round a little so the side of her body was warm against his. The plunge of her neckline exposed her breasts as she turned to look Kunda in the face. Her hand rested on the inside of his thigh.

'Hi Bulongo, I'm Audrey.'

Kunda tried to talk about nothing. He could tell Audrey was getting impatient with him. The third round of drinks arrived. Suddenly the driver downed his and stood up.

'D'ya want her?' the driver asked Kunda, pointing at Audrey. 'No?' he said, as Kunda hesitated. 'Let's go.' He peeled a green fifty off a roll of notes and dropped it on the table. 'That's for the drinks. Next time, maybe.'

The bar had filled. A real mixture. Locals in smart suits, white businessmen in cheap suits, nature guides and managers in from the bush, still wearing safari gear. Many of the guides were either South African or Australian, tanned and out of the bush for the first time in weeks. They were beginning to get rowdy and their tables were becoming crowded with empty bottles. Kunda thought he recognized one of them and quickly looked away. He had been stupid coming to this place, he reprimanded himself.

The driver raced off, even faster than when they had arrived, thumping his fist on the horn each time anyone threatened to cross his path. A joint he had lit hung from his lips, clouding smoke on each breath.

Minutes later they stopped outside the front door of the Seymour International Hotel. The driver got out and tossed the keys to the doorman. Inside was dark and miserable. Kunda had wanted to stay in the bakkie, but the driver had insisted.

'Whisky. And more chicken, big girl she do everything I tell her. From Zaire, you'll like her.'

In the bar there were lots of girls sitting around in groups looking uninterested. A few white men, in jeans, sat at the bar watching football on a snowy TV screen. Kunda guessed the place had seen better days, now frequented mainly by white Europeans working in the Copper Belt and black tradesmen up from South Africa.

The driver slapped the shoulder of the security guard, who was stood watching the football from the doorway, and smiled as he passed. He carried on walking in the direction of a table of girls, snatching the closest by the hair, pulling it and shaking it hard. A bottle on the table tipped over. The security guard turned and wandered out into reception.

'Fucking smile when someone walks in the bar, da'Rwanda.'

Kunda didn't think the gelo came from Rwanda, but guessed the word was used as an insult in Lusaka. As the driver let her go, his jacket puckered at the back and Kunda realized he had a gun stuck in his belt. He was in enough trouble, the last thing he was looking to do was draw attention to himself. Maybe hooking up with these guys had been a mistake. Maybe Romance had been his best bet. But with no mahafu in his pocket, and no longer any identity, he knew laying his hands on some real money fast was what he needed.

'Come, I'm really flat with these gelos, we go somewhere else.' The driver gave him a friendly shove towards the door, but he could feel the anger seething.

'How they think I look after them if they have no mahafu to give me?' Kunda listened to him rant and followed him out front.

They drove around the city for almost two hours, stopping only to roll joints. Back past the Brightwater, out on the Great E towards the airport, round the Castle shopping centre, and round again, and into the Misisi compound, then out past the polo club. The driver did not say where they were going or what they were doing. Kunda hoped it would not end with the driver jumping out with the gun in his hand.

Slowly the urgency drained. They sat in traffic crawling slowly along Cairo Road and turned off down a side street, close to the club where Kunda had taken Jabu what seemed a lifetime ago. Kunda sat and waited to see what the driver would do. He looked over his shoulder and called for Kunda to come on.

'Shake Shake.' The driver pointed to a bar a few doors up.

Inside, the bar was dark and empty except for a couple of guys playing pool on a small table under a single spotlight. Kwaito music played quietly. A few times, the driver's head dropped forward and he sat up again with a start.

Two girls walked in, sat at the bar and looked across. Tight, bright-coloured short dresses stretched over almost flesh-free bodies. The one in green smiled at Kunda.

'Stay clear of them, they heading straight to the

departure lounge,' the driver said without much interest. 'You wanna graze?'

Kunda could not remember the last time he had eaten. Then he could, and he quickly put the moment out of his mind. Drinking had filled him, but he was starving. He nodded. But just as they were going to leave, the driver's team piled in through the door with a couple of gelos in tow, laughing and fooling around.

'Hey, Bulongo. What you doing here?'

'Thought I'd spend some time in the city. Find my way around.' Kunda was pleased to see them. Spending the day with the driver, who seemed wired most of the time, had made Kunda nervous at first. Later, sharing the joints, he had felt the slow, sinking weight of depression. He had wanted to be part of something, but cruising around the city with an armed tsotsi was making him feel bad.

'Whisky,' Kunda told the barman, taking a green from his pocket and paying for the round.

'You got my mahafu?' The man who had lent Kunda twenty dollars in the township confronted him.

Kunda took the last of the money from his pocket and held it out.

'I'll give you the rest in a few days.'

'I lash you twenty. This isn't fifteen.'

'Things tight.'

'Ka nduli.'

Kunda didn't like being accused of showing off when all the time he had no money. But he knew Kambeva was right.

'Sha, you close me out for ten dollars.'

'I lash you the money sha, and then you run off.'

'I stay here, you help me make some money and I pay you fifty greenbacks.' Kunda's proposal appeared to resolve both issues.

'You think I moko-moko?'

Kunda raised his hand to place it on Kambeva's

207

shoulder in a friendly gesture, and smiled.

Kambeva stepped forward and, with a swift sleight of hand, stabbed out a small blade. Kunda felt the jab and stepped back. He took his last cigarette from the packet on the table and walked to the toilet. He lit the smoke, and looked in the mirror at the small tear in his shirt. Unknown to this fugitive, the blade had penetrated his chest and pierced his heart. Kunda flicked the butt into the urinal, collapsed on the tiled floor, and died where he fell.

CHAPTER SIXTEEN

Romance had not been with anyone except Kunda. The hand caressing her breast was smooth, gentle, unexpectedly gentle. His tongue ran across the nipple of her other breast, which immediately turned it hard. She did not know how she had come to be in this man's bed. They had made love late in the afternoon, then slept for a while, satisfied in each other's arms.

He was gone now, but he had asked her to stay.

She had been in need of comfort. But that was not it. She had been in need of warmth, human contact, someone to share what it was she had experienced and what she was facing, but that was not it either. Had Stephen seduced her? Certainly she had drunk a little alcohol with him before it had happened, but she did not feel he had taken advantage. He had been gentle, considerate and spoke words, she admitted, which were pleasurable to hear whispered. She recalled all the times over the last year where he had ensured her wellbeing.

Her mind was certainly confused, more confused now than at any time in her life. But there was one thing she knew. One decision she had taken, and it was only now she recognized it. Whatever her life in the future, if she was to have a life, she wanted to be treated as an equal. Equal to the men of her country, and equal to the foreigners bringing their international brands and ideologies with them. That still did not explain to her why she had decided to make love to Stephen, but she would work that out over time. Time she was unsure she could pledge.

Still thoughtful, she lay naked, looking down at her black body on the white crumpled sheets, damp with their pleasure. She could not believe how much weight she had lost over the past month. All the efforts she had made before Christmas for Kunda; now it was just dropping away. Worry. She could buy new clothes, but her troubles were far from over. She had decisions to make, and if last month was anything to go by she might see another stone disappear. Thin as a razor-blade, kaleza, the desperately skinny, the desperately sick. HIV - was that her fate? She knew she did not want to be dead yet, but she was not prepared to spend the rest of her life looking over her shoulder. Was everything in life just chance, just good luck and bad luck? She considered going to an inkanga, and did not dismiss the idea.

'Romance.'

She had not heard a vehicle pull in, but she heard the door click at the same time as she heard Stephen's voice. Quickly she pulled the covers over herself.

'I thought we might go out and eat,' Stephen suggested, moving into the doorway where she could see him.

Romance did not feel she was ready to face people: she was confused about everything. Even who she was.

'You go and get some food, and I will shower while you're out and then cook my favourite food for you,' Romance offered, hopefully.

'You'll need to give me a list.'

Dry, she picked up her top from the floor where it had been discarded and wondered if Stephen would mind her wearing one of his shirts.

In the wardrobe his clothes hung in an orderly fashion, mostly things she had seen him wearing in the office. In a separate section were white T-shirts, neatly folded and stacked, ready to be packed at a moment's notice. As she lifted one out she uncovered a black revolver. Motionless, she was contemplating what it meant, and what she should do next. She wanted to pick it up, but was afraid to touch it. After a while she replaced the T-shirt, closed the door and slipped into her crumpled top. It wasn't illegal to own a weapon, if you held a police licence, she knew that. She did not imagine Stephen had one of those, though. She couldn't make up her mind whether she should feel scared or safer.

'We could go into the garden and just throw the chicken on the barbecue, if you didn't want to bother.'

'I want to cook for you,' Romance said, with a little more insistence in her voice than she had intended. What she really wanted was something to do. Something to occupy her. She was not sure what her role was, or what she should talk about just sitting in the garden.

Stephen sat at the table, sipping what Romance judged to be a very large whisky from a beer glass filled with ice.

'What's it called?'

'What's what called?'

'The dish.'

'Bobotie with rice. I thought it would make a change from sadza.'

Romance did not know where anything was, but asking questions to find knives, pots, chinois, chopping board, she kept the conversation going. She prepared the ingredients: chopping and frying the chicken pieces with onion, adding curry powder, lemon juice and nuts, soaking the bread, then placing the mixture in a fireproof dish, topping it with whisked egg and milk, before gently sliding it into the oven. Stephen finished his drink and poured another. Still with a small bottle of Coke unfinished, she refused his offer.

'You haven't told me about your trip back. I know you got here OK, but what happened after I left you at Chirundu?' Stephen asked.

'Not a lot. Mike drove me to the airport, handed me over to Thomas who looks after Digby's guests. There wasn't a flight for fourteen hours he could get me a seat on so he was going to book me into a hotel, but I didn't want that. I just sat in his guest lounge, watched TV and slept in the chair,' she told him.

'You should have gone to a hotel. I told Digby I would settle everything with him.'

'The only hotel with any vacancies was the Seymour International, and everyone complains about that place. No, it was alright. The flight was very different from our flight down to the camp: the noise of the engines quieter, and the speed along the runway, very fast.'

'And no problem at this end?' Stephen asked.

'No, Sanjay was there and he spoke to someone on the desk as I came through, then he dropped me at the office.'

When the egg had set and slightly browned, she placed the dish on a mat to protect the table and strained the rice through a flour sieve, not having been able to locate the conical strainer she would normally have used for hot food. And from the fridge she completed her offering with a jug of shandy gaff: a mixture of lager and ginger beer.

They ate dinner at a small table under a mofwe tree as the sun was going down. Stephen complimented her on her cooking and drank most of the bottle of white South African wine he had chilled, forsaking the low alcohol thirst-quencher.

'Did the police stop you when you landed?' This was not really the question she wanted to ask, but that question was working its way to the front of her mouth.

'The pilot spotted a Land Rover sitting between the hangars as we taxied past. I think they were watching us with binos. He deliberately stopped where they could easily

212

see us, and as soon as I was on the runway he taxied back and took off again before I had entered the arrivals lounge. Sanjay is a good man,' Stephen smiled at the subterfuge Sanjay seemed to master as a matter of second nature.

'He is a good person to have as a friend,' Romance agreed, and followed up with the question that had now worked its way onto her lips. 'When the police came to the office for me, why did you think they were looking for you, Stephen?' She looked into his face: she was not sure whether he was aware she was scrutinizing his reaction. And then she felt stupid.

'That detective doesn't like losing. I thought it was him. The last thing I thought was that they were coming for you, so it had to be me.'

Romance could not make up her mind if Stephen had been paranoid, or there were other reasons he was not telling her.

When they had cleared away, she asked Stephen to take her back to the flat: she did not want the men working in the yard to see her arriving with the boss in the morning.

Alone, her mind troubled, she could not sleep. She wished she hadn't come back; or when Stephen suggested he stay, she hadn't refused.

Hanging in her wardrobe was the dress she had bought. On the shelf was the ticket she hadn't used. She thought of Kunda's body, burnt beyond recognition in their car … the money locked in the safe that had caused their argument. Tears rolled down her face, but she did not sob. She just felt a piece of her life had been sucked out of her.

She wanted to focus on her future, the distant future, a new ambition. Her body was anchored in the present and all her thoughts circulated in the past. Life did not stand still; she was who she was. She had been given an education by a Christian group whose ideas she was not sure she believed then, and now believed less. Church, she realized, was little more than a habit. She enjoyed the songs. Praying

213

at home was as much about setting out her wishes as truly believing she was speaking to her Creator, the Creator of this world.

The learning had allowed her to get a job, to buy a car, save for a house that was more than a hut with a straw roof and mud floors. It was progress, but she was not special. She was not looking to escape. This was her country. She was born and would die here, and be proud to have been part of the growth of the nation. Cleansing was a ritual, one of many on which her nation had been built. Whilst she felt disgust for what was demanded of widows, she was not sure she could simply disregard it. If all the ancient laws were swept away, would her country not just become simply a theme park for tourists? And a fast-food outlet for the people it employed?

But what if the laws were wrong, unjust, just a way for powerful old men to hold on to control. Legal marriages had changed women's rights in divorce. She did not know what she was thinking, where her mind was taking her, least of all how these delusions were helping her cope with the problems she faced.

The following morning, when she carried a stack of files into Stephen's office for him to review, he discreetly touched her hand. He could see the lack of sleep creasing around her eyes, and the ends of her lips finding it hard to conjure up a smile.

'Don't be worried, Romance, everything will be fine. I will help you, it'll be OK.'

She knew he meant well, but this was not his country and he didn't understand. It wasn't his fight. She did not say anything in reply, and Stephen realized she was not convinced he could help.

Later, after the office had closed and Romance had gone upstairs, Stephen came to her door and knocked lightly.

'Romance. I've got a message for you.'

Romance opened the door, but did not step back to

allow Stephen to pass. He didn't make a move.

'It was on my desk. A note one of the yardmen scribbled. I don't understand why it was left there, but I didn't see it until I was tidying up.'

Romance took it and read the scrawl:

miss romance. a man called sonkwe came to see you i said youd gone north he say he going north

'I thought you would want to see it.'

The paper quivered in Romance's hand. She wanted to smile and say thank you. But the reality of what was happening took hold. What would have happened if she hadn't been away. Would Sonkwe have dragged her off, if she had refused to go? When he got to the village and found she was not there, would he return? Romance turned, walked slowly back into the room and sat down. Stephen followed.

She looked at his suntanned hand as it covered both hers on the table. He smiled reassuringly. He could be the answer she needed, she thought to herself. He leaned forward and kissed her. She didn't reject his mouth, but barely responded.

'I have to go to Jo'burg for a few days. When I get back we can make a plan,' he told her.

She nodded. She could not think of any kind of plan that would make her problem disappear. For a while she allowed him to take control of her. He went out and returned with a bucket of fried chicken and some drinks. She ate the food he placed in front of her and when he suggested that she would feel better if she had a shower, she took a shower. They made love, but she had no passion to give and more than once she saw Sonkwe and other faces she could barely recollect waiting to take their turn.

Stephen slept. Romance lay awake with his arm stretched across her. She believed Stephen was a good man, but she did not see how he could be the answer, even if it was an answer she could envisage.

She didn't know how quickly the cleansing must happen after the husband dies. She had no idea if the point of the ritual faded if it was not carried out within a set period. One year, five years, twenty years? Before morning she had decided she would go to a sangoma, who would be able to advise her, to look into her future. She would talk to the woman in the market who had sold her the dress. Romance felt she would be someone who knew the best sangoma in the district.

Romance did not hear Stephen leave. After taking her decision she had become relaxed, and drifted into a deep sleep.

o0o

The van bounced; her passenger held on fearfully as Romance swerved to miss a piece of debris in the road. It was the first time she had driven in a year, and she had never been behind the wheel of anything other than a small car.

Stephen had not refused when she had asked to borrow one of the company vehicles. She had declined his offer to drive her wherever it was she wanted to go.

At lunchtime, she had walked to the market and approached the clothes seller. Romance's hunch had been right, but the sangoma with the true wisdom Romance was told she needed lived in the hills fifteen miles to the west of the town. In return for five green notes, the woman had agreed to take Romance if she had her own transport.

They had been driving for forty minutes, the speedo had clocked up twenty-two miles, and each time Romance asked how much further, the woman kept telling her they would be there soon.

At thirty-one miles, the woman pointed to a dirt track

off to the left. Romance had the headlights on main beam, having never driven in the dark before. She was worried they would get hijacked and the company vehicle stolen. After another mile driving at a snail's pace, the woman touched Romance's arm and pointed to a hut a few yards off. It was the only sign of habitation they had seen since leaving the main road. Romance pulled over and parked outside.

'Go in. She will know why you've come. I'll stay here,' the woman said, pushing her as she opened the van door.

Romance was more nervous now than she had been at any time over the last few days. Suddenly, the image of the gun she had seen in Stephen's wardrobe flashed into her head and she wished she had asked to borrow that as well. She looked around: it was impossible to see anything except the dim light glowing behind the curtain door of the hut. There was no noise except the hum of the engine fan. Romance looked back at her passenger, who waved her forward. A stick under her foot cracked as she went, the sound filling the night.

'Come, mwana. Come, child. Don't be afraid.' The voice came from behind the curtain, just as Romance had been about to say 'knock knock'.

She lifted the curtain and looked about her as she stepped forward. It was one large room, spotlessly clean. A woman sat on rush matting in the shadows at the far end.

'Come, mwana. I have been waiting for you. I thought you would come yesterday or the day before. What has taken you so long?' Her voice was soothing.

Romance approached her, and as her eyes became more accustomed the low light, she could see a woman younger than she had expected. Her head-wrap was ornate; a long necklace sparkled as flames from the small fire flickered in the breeze caused by her entrance. On the floor in front of her were a scattering of bones and stone. She indicated for Romance to sit.

Romance's eyes scanned the walls. Behind the woman hung a string of teeth, a leopard-skin and a collection of clubs and sticks. To the side stood a shelved cabinet filled with jars and tins.

'Your hand, mwana.' The woman held out her own and waited for Romance to take it.

Romance watched her examine her palm and then turn her hand and scrutinize her nails, wondering how little the woman could see in such subdued lighting. She squeezed Romance's hand and let it go. From her lap she chose one of two small cloth bags, which Romance had not noticed before.

'The stones, I think.'

The sangoma held it in both hands, then up-ended the cloth; the contents of pebble-smooth stones emptied on the mat between them.

Both women eyed the assorted contents. Romance wondered what they would mean for her.

'You understand the whole of your life is in these stones. The life you have had, and the life you will come to have. What I must decide first is if the bigger stones are your past or your future.'

The room remained silent for a long time.

'You are a very strong woman. Few women in this country have the power to divide the road they walk. If you turn back on yourself, the small stones will be the future. If you have the strength, then the big stones tell me your life will be long and full of plenty.'

'My husband is dead. I should go back to my village. I need to know what will be happening if I don't.'

'Cleansing is a painful thing, for some, for their body and their head. It is more difficult for those who have left their traditional surroundings. But if a woman does not go through this ritual, the ghost of the husband will remain in her. Bad luck for all the family and the widow.'

'Are you saying I should go back?'

'I cannot tell you what you should do, mwana. You must make your own life.'

'You said if I turn back, my life will be the small stone. My life will be short. So I should not go back to my village.'

'Going back may mean keeping the ghost of your husband inside you.'

'And must I marry my brother-in-law as well?'

'Mwana, you are already his property.'

'I would die before I spend my life with him.' Romance felt tears on her cheek, as much from anger as sadness.

'Then maybe you should take a small stone. The large stones are not for everyone. The chief, your headman, will not forget you until you have been cleansed or you pass from this world. Your husband's brother's claim on you is for your husband's brother.'

Again the room remained silent. The journey to the sangoma had been a waste, Romance decided. She wiped her eyes and began to stand.

'Take a stone, child.'

'No.'

The sangoma took a stone from the floor, placed it in the bag and hung it on a hook behind her.

'Twenty green, mwana.'

Romance begrudgingly took the notes from her purse and handed them over. At the door, the woman called her back.

'Take this before his ghost leaves: it will make the memory small small.' The woman handed a twist of paper into which she had spooned a powder from one of her pots.

The drive back seemed shorter, even though neither woman spoke. The market woman had taken troubled people to the sangoma before, and knew afterwards they were in no mood to gossip. The wisdom the sangoma passed on took them to a distant place.

Romance undid the lock, removed the chain on the

gates, and drove into the yard. The whole building was in darkness. She thought Stephen may have waited for her to return, but he hadn't and that pleased her. She wanted to be on her own. During the night, her mind turned over and over.

The following day, Stephen informed her that he would fly to Jo'burg so that he would not be away any longer than was absolutely necessary, and asked her to book him a hire car at the airport, returning Saturday.

'This time I won't forget to leave you the safe key.' He handed her a bunch. 'The key to my place is on there;, if you would feel safer, please stay there while I'm away. You can use one of the pickups to get backwards and forwards. And don't worry, as soon as I get back we'll sit down and figure out what to do for the future. Maybe we could open an office in SA, and you could manage that. That should be far enough to keep you out of harm's way.'

Romance insisted she would be OK. And yes, they could talk when he got back.

Before Stephen left Romance took an envelope, wrote her sister's name and address on the outside, and put half the money she had inside.

'Stephen, I know it's a lot to ask, but if you have time could you drive to where my sister lives, and give her this? It's some money, so please don't leave it if she isn't there. Her husband is away, so he won't give you any trouble.'

'You have my word, if she's there I'll find her,' Stephen promised, squeezing her arm gently before leaving. She felt he had wanted to hug her, but she had stepped slightly back in fear someone would enter the office or see their embrace through the door.

Romance went to Stephen's bungalow each evening, but did not stay. Each time she went to his bedroom and opened the wardrobe. On the first night she looked at the clothing under which the revolver was hidden, but did not touch anything. On the second night, when she returned, she was not sure it would even be there, even if she did lift his clothing. But he had flown; she knew it was difficult to travel on a plane with a weapon. Carefully she took each item away. The gun was still there, but as much as she wanted to pick it up she could not bring herself to do so.

She held it in her hand on the third visit; it was the first time she had held a gun in her hand, and she was shocked at the heaviness. She sat on the floor holding it in both hands, the way she had seen guns held on TV, her arms stretched out between her legs. She lifted her arms out straight and considered what it would be like to squeeze the trigger when someone was standing in front of her. She turned it and held it in both hands, pointing it towards herself. She wondered what size the stone was which the sangoma had picked from the floor and placed in the bag, and she wondered if the woman had taken it from the hook the moment she had left.

The following evening, after locking the office, she did not go to Stephen's; she packed a small bag, took the envelope with the unused ticket in it and the twist of paper the sangoma had given her, and walked slowly to the bus station.

EPILOGUE

On returning to her village, Romance was systematically raped by three of Kunda's relatives. The headman oversaw the 'cleansing', and when the ritual was over he offered her a small piece of scrub land where she could build a hut if she wanted to stay. All her husband's possessions, including his hut, had been taken by his family, along with the money and possessions Romance carried when she arrived at the village.

One week later Stephen came and took her away.

Prudence writes a short letter to her sister Romance a couple of times a year. She left her husband and Jo'burg shortly after Kunda's death, and is living with a man from Zaire who works on the pan-African road construction projects funded by the Chinese. Each letter is postmarked from a different location, and none contain a contact address. Each letter contains an apology for deeds unspecified.

Sonkwe's whereabouts are unknown.

Stephen married an Australian NGO nurse in 2004 and has two children. In the 2009 financial crisis he purchased the business he had managed for some ten years from his boss, Mr Robertson, and is expanding it throughout southern Africa with investment funding from Sanjay Johal.

Two months after Romance had been 'cleansed' she travelled to England and attended an abortion clinic at Stephen's expense. She did not return to work at Krystaal Pool Systems. Instead she took over the running of Kingsley's boat-building and repair business, becoming the sole owner on the death of Kingsley's parents in 2005. She now employs sixteen people and is one of the most successful importers of chemicals, marine spare parts and leisure equipment in that area of Africa. At a conference of business leaders where she was invited to speak, she told her audience that at one time she would ask God to make everything fine, but she had come to realize that in this life you had to be strong and take the rough with the smooth.

In 2006, Romance set up the No Woman No Die charity, providing safe houses for women seeking asylum from the harsh rights still afforded men in a number of southern African countries.

The 'sexual cleansing' ritual has been set aside by many village elders, as AIDS continues to have a tragic consequence throughout the continent; although the public face and the private actions rarely coincide. The practice of 'non-penetration' sex has been accepted as an alternative by many headmen. The fear is that when a cure or reliable treatment for AIDS is found, those with strong tribal allegiances will seek to reinstate the practice.

GLOSSARY

Are you winning?	How's your day going? (informal greeting)
AIDS	Acquired immunodeficiency syndrome
Babbalos	Hangover (slang)
Bakkie	Pickup truck (slang)
Big house	Wife (slang)
Bilharzia	Sickness caused by parasites in stagnant water
Binos	Binoculars (abbreviation)
Black table	Dirty table full of beer bottles (slang)
Bobotie	SA spiced meat dish; Cape Malay origin
Boma	Safe enclosure
Bompie	Fat girl, easily available for sex (slang)
Braai	SA term for barbecue (Afrikaans)
Bulongo	A fighter, someone who will not give up (slang)
Bushmeat	Meat from wild animals such as lion, buck or zebra
Bwana	Boss
Carpaccio	Dish made from finely sliced raw beef (Italian)
Chamba+dusted	Marijuana + other drug possibly heroin (slang)
Chibuku	Local millet beer; opaque, porridge-like consistency
Chicken	Prostitute (slang)
Chi gebenga in Tonga	Untrustworthy person, cheat (slang)
Clunk	Smell (slang)
Chinois	Conical strainer for cooking (French)
Chipo	Woman's name, meaning a gift
Chitenge	Long cotton-wrap dress
Chicken	Prostitute (slang)
Dagga	Marijuana (slang)
Da'Rwanda	Slow-witted; local attitude to Rwandans (slang)
Departure lounge	Waiting to die (of AIDS related illness) (slang)
Duzvi	Excrement (slang)
Flat	Angry (slang)
Fokken doff	Stupid (from Afrikaans)
Gelo	Girl, woman (slang)
Graze	Eat (slang)
Greenback	US dollar (slang)
Half jack	Half bottle of spirit (slang)
HIV	Human immunodeficiency virus
Inkanga	Witch doctor, usually one who casts bad spells
Jabu	Woman's name, meaning joy
Jantar	Portuguese culinary speciality
Kapenta	Very small fish, common in Lake Kariba
Kunda	Man's first name, meaning family man

Kaleza	'Thin as a razor blade'; HIV-infected (slang)
Kwaito	SA music, similar to slow garage or hip-hop
Kak	Excrement (slang)
Kambeva	Nickname meaning small but fast and effective
Ka nduli	Show off, brag (slang)
Kasaka	Bag of money (slang)
Kukhuza	Male voices in grief-stricken wailing at funerals
KWV	Good-quality SA brandy
Lash	Give (slang)
Lekker	Good, tasty (slang)
Lobola	Money or good paid by groom for bride
Maglite ®	Heavy, long-handled torch; used as truncheon
Mahafu	Money (slang)
Moko-moko	Insane or mentally challenged (slang)
Mopani	Caterpillar from mopani tree; source of protein
Mosi	Locally brewed lager
Mwana	Child
Narrow house	Coffin (slang)
Nyaminyami	Mythical river god; three foot long serpent
Praca	Town square (Portuguese)
Renamo	Mozambique white freedom fighters/terrorists
RIB	Rigid inflatable boat
SA	South Africa; South African
Sangoma	Witch doctor; 'white witch', removes bad spells
Sha	Friend (slang)
Shake Shake	Commercially brewed chibuku beer
Shona	Southern African tribe; Bantu language
Shorty	Girl (slang)
Small house	Mistress, unmarried sexual partner (slang)
Smeka	Money (slang)
Strap	Walk (slang)
Sadza	Maize porridge, main item of staple diet
Tight	Difficult (slang)
Tshova	Shared taxi, usually minibus
Tsotsi	Gangster, layabout
Twenty green	Twenty US dollars (slang)
Warried	Relaxed, carefree (slang)
Word up	Speak to (slang)
Zim	Zimbabwe (abbreviation)

AUTHOR'S NOTES:

The country in which Romance resides, the characters, the businesses and the situations in this novel are all fictitious, being the product of the author's imagination. Any similarity to people living or dead is purely coincidental.

The pressures experienced by many young women in Africa today, is true. The lack of understanding by many African politicians regarding the transfer of AIDS is true. The practicing of the sexual act of cleansing is an ancient rite still carried out in many African nations, this is true.

MC

ABOUT THE AUTHOR

Michael Connor is a freelance writer specializing in food, travel and crime issues. He is hotel-school trained and has spent lengthy period in Africa (including Zimbabwe, Zambia and Sierra Leone), China, Greece and the former Republic of Yugoslavia, the Caribbean and the UK.

He has researched and written a full page weekly feature for the Caterer and Hotelkeeper magazine over a six year period, plus a variety of pieces for Now Magazine, GQ, Adrenalin, The Guardian, The Mirror and The News of the World.

Michael Connor is a member of English PEN which promotes free speech, human rights and a greater understanding through literature.

OTHER WORKS BY THE SAME AUTHOR

Biography
The Soho Don (Mainstream Publishing/Random House)

Travel
Place Settings (Ezine)

www.michael-connor.co.uk